MARRYING A SWEET SISTER

BOOK ONE

THE SWEETEST BOND

A.T. BUTLER

THE SWEETEST BOND

Clean Historical Romance of the Frontier

MARRYING A SWEET SISTER

A.T. BUTLER

CHAPTER ONE

Upon stepping from the train onto the platform in Laramie, Wyoming Territory, Jenny Sweet realized she'd been very wrong. Clutching the handle of her carpetbag in one hand, she ran the other hand over her dark brown hair, smoothing it down as she looked around.

The wild, hardy western danger that she'd been bracing for was nowhere to be seen. This frontier train station was far from the messy, backward cesspool she'd expected. Instead, everywhere she looked were well-dressed women being welcomed home by loving husbands, uniformed porters transporting luggage, hired carriages calling for customers. There was even a small food cart at the far end of the platform from which came the smell of roasting chestnuts; they could be a tempting warmth and needed sustenance after her extensive journey.

She had been riding the Union Pacific railroad for the previous six days from Baltimore, through Chicago, and now on to the wild plains. Though she'd had the chance to stretch her legs and breathe fresh air several times over the trip from back East, now that her journey was finally ended she felt a boost in her mood that had not been there before. Leaving her old life behind made her feel as though a weight had been lifted.

There was a crisp wind, bringing the cold air down from the snow-capped mountains. The town of Laramie was not nearly as large as Baltimore, but somehow it seemed busier. The rugged newness of the frontier invigorated her in ways she did not expect, being used to the old, staid community of an eastern metropolis. That city had been around for more than a hundred and fifty years, and it showed in everything from the worn cobblestone to the firmly entrenched politicians.

She desperately hoped that taking this new position in this frontier territory could be exactly the fresh start that she needed, with none of the previous generations' expectations and the well-meaning criticism of friends that had so plagued her back East. Jenny had thought that she was reconciling herself to relative barbarism in order to embark on this new start, but now, looking around at this cozy town, she realized her expectations had been utterly incorrect.

And she was delighted.

She had accepted a position as a nanny and house-keeper for a widower and his daughter in a small frontier town in the Wyoming Territory. Her sister had almost convinced her to carry a small pistol on her person to protect herself while traveling, but Jenny had never felt comfortable with that kind of tool to damage another person. She'd been a nurse for almost a decade and her instinct was only ever to heal, to help, to offer support. The closest she could ever come to shooting someone would be to instead talk sternly to them—hardly a defense against a bandit or ruffian out on the wild frontier.

In all her years working in medicine, Jenny had found that the more firmly she could state her preference, the more articulately she could offer guidance and instruction, the better for everyone around. Though some people found her forthrightness to be abrasive, Jenny had learned the hard way that letting other people walk all over her would only make her miserable and not especially help the other person. She didn't back down and she didn't obfuscate. This single journey from Baltimore was the only time in her life that she had retreated. As the oldest of four sisters, she'd had more than her fair share of situations in which she needed to make herself heard in no uncertain manner.

And so, as she looked around the train platform for some sign of her new employer, Jenny wondered what her options were should Mr. Garrett not appear for some reason. While a couple of the hired carriages had already disappeared, there seemed to still be options. She would need to inquire specifically where Prairie Winds Ranch was and see that her trunk made it out there, but Jenny had faith that she could figure it out if she had to.

"Miss Sweet?"

She turned at the sound of the low, rumbling voice. The tall, broad-shouldered man standing at the far end of the train platform was looking at her with such intensity in his blue eyes that Jenny almost checked herself over to make sure there was not a button undone, that the bottom ruff of her petticoat was not showing. He closed the distance to her in just a few long strides and immediately reached for her carpetbag.

"I'll take that," he said gruffly. "Come on."

"Wait!"

Jenny took a step back, away from this man who had so taken charge of the entire situation without waiting for her acknowledgment, let alone consent. She yanked her carpetbag out of his reach and held her other hand up to stop him.

"If you are Lucas Garrett, could we at least have some semblance of a polite introduction before you put your hands on my belongings? And if you are not Lucas Garrett, then I'm sorry, sir, but I will not be going anywhere with you."

The man huffed, clenching his jaw in frustration and not taking his eyes off of her. Jenny simply stared back at him in turn. When she had accepted this position to be nanny and housekeeper for a widowed rancher, she had no idea part of her responsibilities would also be to teach the man manners.

He was in dire need of a barber; his thick dark hair was flecked with gray at the temples, curling around his collar and falling into his eyes. While his attire—denim, chambray, sheepskin coat layered against the late winter chill—seemed clean, it also appeared well-worn, as though he lived in these clothes.

Not that she expected her employer to dress formally when he came to collect her from the train, but she would have thought that some small amount of effort was called for. This was their very first introduction, and would set the tone for the rest of their time together.

But then, she reminded herself, this was precisely what she'd expected of her new life on the frontier—casual chaos, survival, and lowered standards. She would just have to do the best she could with what God had given her.

———

Lucas knew that losing his temper at this woman to whom he had not even introduced himself would be more trouble than it was worth, so he held his jaw tight as he calmed his breathing. Dressed as she was in layers of satin and edging of lace and ribbon and whatnot, in those delicate black boots with low heels, told him all he needed to know—this woman had no proper idea how to survive on a ranch and no concept of what it meant for him to be away from his land for long enough to meet the train.

Her hair was thick and dark, like his own, but somehow warmer and softer. It was pulled off her face in some practical hairstyle he could not name, pinned up under her flat straw hat. While her expression was frank and open, Lucas could not help but feel as though she was not going to be the motherly character that faded into the background that he'd wished for.

While he had initially engaged a nanny and housekeeper for his home—the Prairie Winds Ranch—because Mary was getting to the age that she needed a guiding feminine hand, he didn't know what to expect, especially from a city woman. Ever since his wife had died, Lucas had made do as best he could. Hiring a stranger from the East was an experiment that he expected to fail. In fact, he would not have given in at all if Mrs. Potter had not insisted, wearing him down over almost a year of coaxing.

"I won't be around forever," she had told him one evening late last summer.

He'd hired her son, Allan, several years earlier to help with tending to the herd, and it only took a couple weeks of Lucas's cooking for Allan to suggest hiring his mother. A widow with no more children at home, Mrs. Potter had been happy to step in to keep house for Lucas and his young daughter. But she was already getting on in years when she came to Prairie Winds Ranch, and periodically she would remind him that he would want to look to the future. There were things she flatly refused to do, reminding Lucas each time that he could find someone younger and stronger and she would take no offense.

It was usually a short conversation. Every few months, she'd say her piece, and he would nod, agree, and then go on about his business without giving it a second thought. The old woman would remind Lucas where she was finding the work more difficult, even while continuing to keep house just fine. He'd been especially grateful for the older woman's kindness and gentle hand with his daughter. She took care of whatever parenting or domestic issues were most pressing, but she could not get to everything. One of the ranch hands would need to carry whatever water she needed, and she regularly retired for the evening before Mary had been put to bed. Lucas and Mary had always made do, but as she got older he realized his daughter deserved better.

The previous summer, however, Mrs. Potter was helping fit Mary with a new dress for the upcoming winter. And when the older woman had accidentally cut a jagged line in the fabric, letting almost a full yard go to waste because her arthritic hands were not strong enough, Lucas finally started to pay attention. He'd finally seen that with her age, with her energy, with her growing frailty, more and more of the tasks around the house were being left unattended to.

"You know, Mr. Garrett," she'd said as she unpinned the ruined fabric from Mary's slight frame. "There are plenty of women in Juniper Falls and beyond who are more than capable of doing things like this."

"I'm not getting married again," Lucas had said sullenly, trying to ward off her argument.

"Of course not," she agreed. "You're far too grumpy to entice any woman in this town."

He thought to take offense at that, but smiled despite himself, recognizing the truth of her words.

"What I had in mind," she continued, "was offering a paid position. Replace me with another hired hand. Bring in a professional for whom you can set proper expectations. She will do her job, you do yours, and there need not be any other fraternization between you, all while Mary gets the hands-on training and guidance that a girl her age needs."

It had been the same refrain that Mrs. Potter had brought up time and time again, but this time Lucas actually listened. He never would have insulted his housekeeper by implying she was too old to work, but with her insistence—not to mention the price of the wasted fabric—he felt like this was a necessary change.

The next day, he sent a telegram to place ads in several of the big metropolitan newspapers. In it he was very clear what qualifications he required and what he was offering. What convinced him to hire Miss Sweet was the fact that she was a nurse and, being in her late twenties, so long past any blush of youth that would have illusions about romance. Still, he hadn't been looking forward to it, and just wanted the whole thing over with.

Now, with Miss Jenny Sweet standing in front of him, Lucas regretted all of his choices. He'd looked for a strong woman who he could respect and trust to get things done, and now found himself employing a woman who was strong enough to not simply give in to whatever he wanted. But it was too late now. He had agreed to retain her services for six months, which meant he was responsible for feeding and housing her until the beginning of September.

"Fine," he grumbled finally. He held out his hand, stiffly awkward. "Lucas Garrett of Prairie Winds Ranch, here to ensure Miss Jenny Sweet made it off of the train from Baltimore."

She took his hand and offered him a warm smile; despite himself, he was impressed by the strength and confidence in her grip.

"It's a pleasure to meet you. Miss Jenny Sweet, on my way to Prairie Winds Ranch for the next six months."

They stared at each other for another long moment, each silently daring the other to be the first to give in.

Finally, Lucas could no longer stand the delay—he still planned to check on the herd that was out grazing in the farthest field that day, and they would be losing light if he waited much longer.

"Wagon is this way," he said. "You want to give me that bag now, or is it attached to your hand?"

CHAPTER TWO

"Wagon is this way," he said to Jenny.

"Thank you ever so much," she managed to get out before he turned his back to her and led the way, leaving her alone on the train platform.

Jenny had allowed Mr. Garrett to take her carpetbag, resolving to praise and reward his polite behavior whenever it occurred, no matter how infrequent. In their correspondence over the previous six months, after she'd applied for the position, he had made clear the situation she'd be walking into. His wife had died several years earlier and he had been raising his daughter on his own, with the help of a housekeeper who was no longer up for the long hours and physical demands of the position. To Jenny, that sounded an awful lot like the kind of isolated, harsh environment that could lead a man to forget his manners. Anyone's civility could break down under stress—as she well knew from her years working at the hospital. Maybe all Mr. Garrett needed was a little patience and a little assistance. She could offer that to him, surely. Especially if it meant giving his little girl a safe and comfortable upbringing.

The wagon that he led her to seemed solid and safe, though without even a shred of the allowances for comfort to which she was accustomed. Wisely choosing to hold her tongue, she accepted Mr. Garrett's help in climbing up onto the seat. He stowed her bag in the back of the wagon and returned to the depot to see about her trunk. Though her contract was only for six months of work, Jenny had hoped to make the move permanent, and so had brought all of her possessions to Wyoming. If not at the ranch, perhaps she could find another home in Juniper Falls or even elsewhere in the territory.

One thing was certain—Jenny Sweet would not be returning to Baltimore. Nothing and no one—not even her three sisters—could induce her to go back. There were too many difficult memories tied up with every inch of that city. And too many friends—and former friends—that would not allow her to forget. Her younger sisters had protested her leaving, but ultimately understood. Eliza, in particular, was the first to voice her support of Jenny's plan, always one to encourage an adventure.

All told, despite the rugged landscape, the cranky employer and the distance from museums, culture and family that she had grown up with, Jenny was determined to make this new start on the western frontier successful.

There was nothing she wanted to return to.

The ride to Mr. Garrett's ranch was several hours— far longer than Jenny had expected. In the eastern states, cities were so close together she could have almost gotten from Baltimore to Washington in the time it took them to get from Laramie to the ranch. Out here there was far more space to spread out. As if to add to the dull welcome, Mr. Garrett remained mostly silent the entire time. She tried to engage him with questions about his daughter, about Juniper Falls, about life on the ranch and what she could expect, but his responses were so monosyllabic that she soon abandoned the effort.

It was no matter; with the rolling countryside stretching out in all directions, Jenny had plenty to keep her occupied as they bumped along the ruts and uneven dirt road.

"Is it always this bumpy?" she asked, after the third time jarring her elbow against the side. "Surely that can't be good for the wagon."

"The snow only just melted a week ago,' he stated, not taking his eyes from the road. "Once we can be sure the rain is done, each man will grade the road in front of his ranch. No point in doing it when the wet will just wash it out again."

The uneven motion would make her ill if she allowed herself to pay much attention to it, so instead she busied herself noticing everything she could about the Wyoming Territory. Every few miles they passed a big, wide gate, some standing on their own, some with fences extending into the prairie and elaborate signs announcing *Morris Family Three-Star Ranch* or *Broken Arrow Ranch* or some other proud family's holdings. Most of the ranch homes were set far enough back from the road that she never saw them, but the occasional wisp of fireplace smoke over a grove of trees and peek of a worn roof barn over a hill gave them away.

She wondered how close their nearest neighbor was, how close the town of Juniper Falls would be to her new home. Jenny had a vague idea that Mr. Garrett had at least a couple of ranch hands living on his land, but otherwise she had no earthly concept of how isolated she would be at Prairie Winds Ranch. She didn't even know how often someone would need to go into town for mail, supplies, and other necessities. She was completely unused to rural life.

The Sweet family had lived in Baltimore for several generations, and though she had distant cousins who had spread out throughout Maryland and Virginia, she was most used to the tight, noisy living of row houses. Sharing walls with the family of six next door. Walking the half a mile to the hospital where she worked and would come into contact with dozens of people every day. This living on the prairie would take some getting used to, but as Jenny had never experienced anything quite like it, she was hopeful that it would at least be an interesting adventure.

"You'll be able to hear yourself think," her sister Abigail had said, a bit wistfully.

Jenny smiled to herself as she recognized the sounds of birds chirping from several directions. Somehow, here in the rural West, the scent of cow manure seemed strangely comforting, as though everything was as it should be, a contrast to the offensive stench that wafted from filthy corners in the cobbled streets of the city.

For not the first time, Jenny hoped fervently that all of this would work out.

After a long morning of strained conversation and jostling, Mr. Garrett finally turned the wagon off the main road, through an open gate and up the dirt track toward the ranch house and outbuildings, most of which she could not readily identify. The home and barn were nestled in a small level area backed by low, rolling hills that stretched toward the horizon. Both buildings were a faded gray, the former with dirty green shutters and a matching front door. The roof of the barn looked patched, and the front door of the house bore scuffs and dents from years of abuse. But there were also happy chickens walking around the low grass by their coop and cozy rocking chairs adorning the front porch.

Everywhere she looked were signs that this home was both well-worn and loved. Though Jenny knew nothing about what was required to keep a ranch of this size working, she knew that it must be an enormous undertaking for one person, even for the most experienced rancher. She wondered how even two ranch hands could be enough. When she had worked at the hospital in Baltimore, it had never ceased to amaze her how quickly the systems to keep folks healthy and taken care of broke down when one nurse was missing, when one doctor was running late.

No wonder Mr. Garrett had been so adamant about returning to the ranch right away.

"We'll need supper ready at six for six people," he was saying as he reined in the horses and brought the wagon to a stop.

It took Jenny a long moment to remember that she was now in charge of that. "Oh, yes. Of course. Six people."

"I'll show you to your room and around the house, but then I've got to see to the herd on the far side of the pasture. You can settle in on your own."

"Um. Yes, sir."

She was used to things being sprung upon her—assisting with an emergency amputation, for example, or an orphaned baby abandoned at the hospital door—but she always had what she needed to get the job done. Now, she did not even know what food was in the house, let alone where she could find the kitchen.

Jenny took a deep breath, reminding herself that she was nothing if not resourceful. Mr. Garrett kept her carpetbag in hand as he glanced back to make sure she was following him into the house. She walked up the couple steps to the porch and then through the front door, stepping into the big living room after him and taking in the sight of her new home.

The front door opened directly into the middle of a large living area, with an enormous fireplace straight ahead. Comfortable looking chairs and a settee circled the crackling fire, with other cozy touches—lap blanket, side tables, oil lamps—scattered elsewhere through the room. There was the door to a hallway on her left, and two closed doors and a wide entry to a dining room along the wall to her right. This would be her home for the next six months at least, and she could not wait to settle in, maybe work on her needlepoint by the fire.

She spotted movement at the doorway to the hall, but whoever was there lurked in the shadows.

"Mary," Mr. Garrett said, softening for the first time since Jenny had met him. "Come meet Miss Sweet, please."

A slight, brown-haired, green-eyed girl of about five years old stepped out of the shadows only a foot into the light of the living room. She clutched a worn doll to her chest. Jenny wondered how much of the girl's shyness was tied to her motherless upbringing.

"Hello," Jenny said softly, squatting down to be on Mary's eye-level. "My name is Miss Sweet. What's yours?"

"Mary," the girl replied, though did not come any closer.

Jenny looked up to Mr. Garrett and then again to the girl. "And, Mary, do you know why I'm here?"

She nodded.

"I'm very much looking forward to being your friend, if that's all right with you."

Mary shrugged and looked down at the top of her doll's head.

Jenny's heart broke for the sweet thing, and she hoped that perhaps offering the child some stability would help her blossom.

———

Watching Miss Sweet interact with his daughter, Lucas again felt his temper flare. He wanted to step between them. How had he managed to find the one woman who somehow knew every tiny thing that irritated him?

"You're not here to be her friend," he said coldly to his new housekeeper. "Do not go putting such ideas in her head."

"Oh!" Miss Sweet looked startled as she stood again. "Well— Then— I suppose, my apologies."

She looked as though she wanted to say more, but Lucas didn't want to hear it.

"We will deal with expectations and requirements later," he said, still gripping the handle of her carpetbag tightly. "Let me show you to your room."

He plowed forward without waiting for her response, driving himself directly between the woman and the girl as he led the way down the hall. She would either follow him or she would not.

The Garrett house had been built as just a single room twenty years ago, when the ranch was first being settled. What had once been the kitchen space was now the big fireplace in the living room. A bachelor, John Swenson looking to avoid the war between the states, had traveled to the Wyoming Territory and put down roots. Lucas himself had come West immediately after the war with his bride Christine and found work at Prairie Winds Ranch. He and Christine helped build the ranch into what it was today, and when Swenson had died unexpectedly just two years after the Garretts arrived, Lucas was shocked and honored to learn everything had been left to them.

Over the next several years, Lucas and Christine poured everything they had—time, money, strength— into improving the ranch and expanding the house. Mary had come along, but afterward Christine never regained her strength. When his wife died, leaving him with only his grief and a three-year-old Mary, Lucas distracted himself by putting even more work into the house, the outbuildings, the land and herds. The enormous living room was the heart of the house, with a big old-fashioned fireplace to keep the space warm. On one side of the room was the kitchen, dining room, his office and bedroom; on the other side was the longer hallway to three more bedrooms where Mary, Mrs. Potter, and now Miss Sweet would be staying.

It was down this hallway that he now strode, trusting that Miss Sweet would follow.

He stopped at the middle door and flung it open, tromping into her room without ceremony and dropping the carpetbag on the bed.

"I'll have the boys bring your trunk in sometime this afternoon," he said, without checking to see if she was close enough to hear. He threw open the curtains and pushed open the window, letting in all the cold, early-spring air. "Your room is next to Mary's in case she needs you in the night. Now—"

He turned back to the door to see Miss Sweet standing in the hallway, her eyes wide as she watched him. Lucas frowned; she would need to get better at keeping up.

"Now, let me show you the kitchen and then I've got to get back to work. Mrs. Potter can answer any more of your questions."

He stepped past her and strode back down the hallway, eager to get this part over with.

CHAPTER THREE

Her employer strode purposefully down the hallway and away from her, leading her across the living room.

"Wait! But— Oh! Mrs. Potter?" Jenny stammered as she hurried to catch up with Mr. Garrett. "Forgive me, but I thought I was replacing Mrs. Potter."

"You are," he said over his shoulder, "but you don't expect me to just throw an old woman who gave me her best service out in the snow, do you?"

"I— I suppose not, no." This was a tenderness she never would have expected from such a prickly man.

Jenny thought quickly as they reached the living room and crossed it to the doorway on the other side. This was all going so fast, and for all she knew he would be cross with her if she missed even the smallest detail. While she'd often received rapid-fire instructions as a nurse, with all the new people and places and expectations, she'd hoped this settling in to a new home could go more slowly. She hadn't eaten in hours, and her joints were still a bit stiff from sitting for so many days. As

Jenny followed Mr. Garrett, she tripped lightly on the edge of the braided rug that was in the entrance, but caught herself before she fell, certain he would not stop for her.

Mr. Garrett didn't even glance back at the sound of her stumbling; he disappeared through the open doorway. Pausing to steel herself, Jenny took a deep breath, squared her shoulders and stepped into the dining room . . .

Which was empty of people.

Shaking her head at herself, Jenny crossed the room to the next doorway, drawn by the smell of freshly baked bread. When she entered the kitchen, she saw an old woman with soft fluffs of white hair. The woman, who could only be Mrs. Potter, was drying dishes. Mary sat at the small kitchen table, her doll in her lap, and Mr. Garrett stood awkwardly in the middle of the room. He seemed almost too big for the space, and Jenny felt a surge of gratitude that she would be living under the roof and protection of such a strong man.

"Take your time looking around?" he asked when he saw her.

"No, I— I'm sorry, I—"

"Never mind. You'll have plenty of time. You should . . . feel at home, I suppose."

Jenny thought those words must have been dragged out of him. It was a good thing, for her own sake, that she had not arrived expecting warm hospitality. Having three younger sisters who all needed attention did that to a person. She certainly could not look for that here. She was in Juniper Falls to do a job, and to care for this little girl. Any thought of her own comfort was sheer frivolity.

"Thank you." She hoped that her own calm and warmth would lure him to exhibit something close to the same, but given his behavior so far, she feared it was in vain. "Shall we have some tea and get to know each other a little bit?" Jenny suggested, looking from Mary to her father and back again. "I'm happy to tell you about myself a bit more, and you can tell me all your plans for the summer, and for the ranch?"

Mary looked down at the doll in her lap.

————

Lucas watched his shy daughter, wishing for the hundredth time that her mother was still around. This child was growing up, and he had no idea what a girl needed. At times, Lucas felt as though his heart literally ached with his desire to do the best he could for Mary, for Christine's sake as well as for her own. He still blamed himself for her death—he should have kept her off her feet, had doctors from every city. He did not want to regret Mary's upbringing as well.

Where other men might resent their children for costing their wife's life, their unique circumstance only made Lucas cherish Mary even more tightly. She only had him, after all, and no child should have to grow up without at least one loving parent. When Christine had first died two years earlier, he had gone through the motions of keeping Mary fed and warm, but had barely interacted with her at all. Once he had begun to notice that lack of interaction affecting her development, he wanted to do everything he could to reverse it before it was too late.

This became yet another task to give his attention to, and focusing on everything other than himself meant that his grieving and heartbreak had lasted far longer than another widower's might. Even now, he could not imagine opening up to another person; an employee who knew how he took his coffee and changed his sheets was the most intimacy he would allow.

Sitting at the kitchen table, Mary had remained silent through this entire interaction. He could tell from the way that she was fidgeting—rubbing the fingertips of her doll's hand—that Mary was interested in this new woman. While he could not sit and have tea—there was still so much to do—perhaps it would be a good thing for the little girl.

"Mrs. Potter, you can take care of that, can't you?" he asked, turning toward the older woman. "Show Miss Sweet where everything is. Answer her questions. Mary can have a couple of cookies with her tea, but I have to get back to the animals. I've been away too long already."

"Of course, Mr. Garrett." Mrs. Potter was already filling the kettle with water. "You just leave it to me and we'll get Miss Sweet settled in. We'll see you at supper."

"Supper at six. For all six of us," he reminded them. Lucas put a hand on his daughter's small, delicate shoulder as he squatted down to her eye level. "Miss Sweet and Mrs. Potter will spend the afternoon with you, pet. But I'll see you in a few hours, all right? You'll be good?"

Mary nodded, eyes darting past him to look at Miss Sweet again.

"Yes, Papa."

He kissed her cheek, resting his big, work-worn hand on the top of her head as he stood again. Mary's dark hair was an exact match to her mother's, soft and straight closer to her skull before spreading out in an unruly mane of curls as it reached her shoulders. Mrs. Potter tried to rein it in—to keep it out of the little girl's way when she played if nothing else—but Lucas always loved to see it hanging loose about her heart-shaped face. While he couldn't stop the passage of time, he could help his daughter stay young, innocent, and free of the concerns of the grown-up world as long as possible.

"All right, then," he said, looking around at the kitchen again.

Mrs. Potter wordlessly handed him a canteen and half a sandwich wrapped in a handkerchief. He would certainly forget to eat if she was not there every day to remind him. He nodded his thanks and turned to Miss Sweet.

"I, uh . . ." He could feel Mrs. Potter's gaze on him, willing him to be polite to this woman who had traveled almost two thousand miles to help him and his family. "I hope you will be very happy here, Miss Sweet."

"Thank you."

He could not read the expression on her face, but he didn't try to. It didn't matter if she was the best cook in the world or merely managed to not poison them. It didn't matter that she was young and vibrant, with the kind of soft smile that made him wonder what would make her laugh, or if she was as withered as an old hag. What mattered was how Miss Sweet looked after Mary. Everything else—including details like showing her the location of the cellar door—was incidental.

She would learn soon enough what his priorities were. Or Mrs. Potter would tell her.

Looping the strap of his canteen over his shoulder, Lucas headed back through the dining room to the front door and outside again. The early spring weather was crisp, and he could already feel the cold stinging his cheeks. It was precisely the kind of weather that he loved for working outdoors; he could exert himself, push himself to his physical limits and not get too hot.

When Lucas reached the grass just off his porch, he noticed with pleasure that Teddy or Allan had taken care of the wagon and horses. Miss Sweet's trunk still sat on the porch by the door, but the important bit—the animals—had been seen to. He wondered if one of them had had a chance to check on the herd in the far pasture, or if they were waiting for his return. Putting his new housekeeper out of his mind entirely, Lucas went to find his ranch hands.

As he crossed his land, Lucas made note of all the other springtime projects they would need to get started. Just as he'd explained to Miss Sweet about the ruts in the road, there was little point trying to make any progress on outdoor projects until the snow melted for the season. He remembered her bafflement at the conditions of the road. Such city ignorance. But he was resigned—she would take care of whatever needed to happen indoors and he would take care of all the rest. Miss Sweet would make sure that his daughter had a safe and supportive home, and that was what mattered. He told himself not to think about her anymore.

———

As Jenny watched her employer leave, she felt a bit let down. It was not as though she'd expected Mr. Garrett to be thrilled to befriend her or to spend all sorts of time with her, but she had hoped that at least on her first day he could make time to get to know her. They would be living under the same roof, caring for the same child. For goodness' sake, she would be doing his laundry and making his meals—why would he not want to at least have a conversation with a person that intimately connected to his family?

Jenny didn't understand it, but at least she had Mary and Mrs. Potter to help her get settled.

"While the water is heating," the older woman said, over the sound of Mr. Garrett closing the front door, "why don't I show you around the kitchen?"

"That would be— Thank you. Yes, please. And I'm so sorry if I am intruding on your . . . space or livelihood. I assure you, I had no idea that you would still be here when I arrived."

"Oh, honey, not to worry." Mrs. Potter opened the kitchen door that led outside. "Mr. Garrett is far easier to get along with than it may seem today. I'm sure everything will work out. We'll find our pace. I'll tell you all about it sometime. But first . . ."

They left the kitchen door open and walked outside just a few steps. Mrs. Potter pointed out the well, the smokehouse, and the chicken coop.

"Everything else," she explained, "the boys will take care of. Milking is always in the morning, and they'll bring the buckets into the kitchen for you to take care of. I usually check the nesting boxes for eggs once each morning, though Mary is getting old enough to start taking on that chore soon. Any butchering or hunting is usually done in the afternoons. Every day is different at Prairie Winds Ranch, and yet there's a kind of rhythm to it. You'll see."

She led the way back to the kitchen.

"It was like that working at the hospital," Jenny said as she followed her back indoors. "There could be seven different emergencies or illnesses, and yet they seemed to need the same treatment as the ones we saw the previous week."

"Fortunately," Mrs. Potter said, moving to the cupboards, "there are significantly fewer life and death emergencies here than you had in the hospital. Not *none,* mind you. But fewer."

"Thank goodness for that," Jenny said. "How can I help?"

Mrs. Potter pulled down teacups, saucers and plates while pointing out the cookie jar to Jenny. Mary watched them both with wide eyes, a smile creeping on to her face when she saw the sweets. In addition to their tea and cookies, they gathered bread and jam, carrot sticks, and cheese sandwiches.

"I imagine you must be quite hungry after your travels," Mrs. Potter said as she finally sat. "Please tell me that Mr. Garrett made sure to get you a lunch before you left Laramie."

Jenny's stomach growled. "He did not," she said with

a laugh. "There was a vendor selling roasted chestnuts on the train platform. I should have gotten some before we left, but I had no idea what a long ride it would be."

"Mr. Garrett has a head for details only if they pertain to his animals. He's not unkind . . . he's just a bit . . ."

"He seems like a very focused man," Jenny offered.

Mrs. Potter glanced at Mary. "Little pitchers have big ears."

"Why don't you tell me about yourself?" Jenny asked, changing the subject. She took a bite of her shortbread.

Mrs. Potter nodded. "You eat. I can talk well enough."

With that, Jenny picked up one of the sandwiches. She slumped back into her chair, resolved to appreciate what might be the last moment of someone else looking after her while she had it.

CHAPTER FOUR

The crisp air stung Jenny's lungs. She'd grown up close enough to the sea that the dry air of winter had never really bothered her. Now, though, on the Great Plains with the wind coursing over the vast expanse of continent, the cold felt different. Sharper, somehow. Mrs. Potter had told her to expect another week or two of cold weather, but that any day now they should be seeing the green sprouts and stalks poking up out of the earth.

"As soon as the ground thaws," the older woman had told her, "you'll need to get one of the boys to help put in the vegetable garden."

The list of things that Mrs. Potter made clear were now Jenny's responsibility seemed to grow by the hour.

She had been at Prairie Winds Ranch for three days now and thought she was starting to get a handle on how it all worked. That first afternoon, in the kitchen over tea and sandwiches, she had peppered Mrs. Potter with questions about the home, the ranch, and—once Mary had gone to her room to play—about the Garrett family.

It was clear that the older woman was guarding the family's privacy when Jenny's questions veered too personal, but even with that barrier she was beginning to feel as though she knew the place.

As well as could be expected after only three days, at least. She still had a lot to learn, both about the way that the ranch worked as well as what was expected of her. Over the previous days, she'd gotten the impression that Mrs. Potter was not in the least threatened by Jenny's being there, and in fact would be looking forward to having far less work to do. Though she had made supper that first night—showing Jenny every step—she'd not made another meal and appeared at breakfast the next morning expecting to be fed just as the boys did.

Jenny found herself not only grateful for the older woman's help and guidance, but also for her friendship. Just as she'd expected the Wyoming Territory to be a land of lawless chaos, she'd also expected to feel very alone in her new home. While there was certainly nowhere near the social engagement and invitations that she'd been blessed with in Baltimore, the ranch was far from desolate. In addition to Mr. Garrett, his daughter Mary, and Mrs. Potter, there were also two young men living on the ranch—Teddy Collins and Allan Potter—who were often referred to as "the boys." The ranch hands had their own bunkhouse closer to the barn, but ate with the family at breakfast and supper.

"Feeding them is all you need to worry about," Mrs. Potter had explained that first night. "I'm sure they'd be grateful for any laundry or sewing repairs or other little comforts you can offer them, but don't feel as though you have to. I certainly never have, even if one of them is my son. They've both taken their laundry into Juniper Falls in the past, or even paid me a few pennies for my assistance. The only thing you absolutely are responsible for is Mr. Garrett's home and Mary's health and happiness."

The ranch hands were both men in their early twenties, full of energy and big plans for their futures. That first night at supper, when Jenny had met them, Teddy had teased and flirted with Jenny as only a boy can when he knows the girl won't take it seriously. He was at least six or seven years younger than her, and seemed to take great delight in entertaining everyone seated at the table. Allan was more somber, but clearly had a good head on his shoulders and was often the one to quietly rein in Teddy's antics.

This early afternoon, she'd had a chance to take a small break from her chores and explore outdoors a bit. When she stepped onto the porch, her eyes lit on Allan and Teddy near the edge of the paddock. They seemed to be repairing the fence that kept the cattle grazing acres separate from the barnyard where the rest of the livestock resided. When Jenny had gotten a flying tour of the ranch that first afternoon, she'd hoped to be able to spend a little more time outdoors. Living in such close proximity to such wide-open spaces was a new adventure for her, and if this position didn't last any longer than her six-month contract, she wanted to be able to say that she'd had the full rural, ranching experience.

She had only thirty minutes or so before she had to get back inside and put her bread in the oven. There was a big pot of stew simmering over low heat, Mary was quietly stringing big wooden beads and buttons onto thread in her room, and Jenny could walk away for a little bit. She walked down the porch steps, crossing the bare dirt to where Teddy and Allan were working. The ground was muddy, so she lifted the hem of her skirt above it, stepping carefully to avoid the worst of the muck.

The dry air smelled pleasantly of a bonfire. Jenny smiled. Every bit of this new life was so different from the life she'd escaped in Baltimore. She was so grateful she'd found this opportunity.

"Come to help?" Teddy asked when he saw her. "You don't have enough to do in the warmth of the ranch house?"

"Teddy, focus," Allan said sharply, not taking his eyes from the fence in front of him.

At a glance, Jenny thought it looked as though they were almost done. They needed to fit the cross piece into the vertical piece—whatever they were called—but with the tension to hold the whole thing in place. She imagined there must be some trick to slipping the pieces past each other, and was suddenly glad that her duties included things like churning butter and canning tomatoes, not building whole structures.

"Just taking a little break to walk around my new home," she said, stopping some five feet away so she wasn't too close. "Remind me—what are the horses names again?"

"Lacey is the filly. Bo is the gelding. Flibbit is the mare," Teddy said.

Jenny laughed. "Flibbit?"

"Mary named her when Mr. Garrett bought her a

year ago," Teddy said as he turned his attention back to the fence. He was holding the post in place while Allan maneuvered the rest of it. "If you can wait another few minutes, I was just going over there to check their feet. You can say hello to them properly."

"I'd love that. Do the pigs have names?"

"Not officially. Sometimes we'll call them Sausage or Pork Chop or something like that. Mr. Garrett is wary of Mary getting too attached to them. Last summer, there was a rooster that he had to let die of old age because Mary would sob anytime he suggested butchering."

"Oh, goodness, that poor child," Jenny said with a laugh. "The only pet I ever had growing up was a cat, and she stayed outdoors just as much as in."

He grinned up at her, but before Teddy could respond disaster struck. Though Allan had kept his focus on his task, holding the split log that was to be fit into the snug hole drilled into the fence, his strength was not quite enough. As Teddy had held the fence post still, Allan shifted his weight. His feet had slipped in the mud, sending him tumbling forward into the fence post, then thudding into Teddy, all but impaling him.

The split log that was to make the fence rail was not sharp—thank heavens—but it wasn't exactly a feather pillow. When the end of the rail rammed into Teddy's side, he cried out and fell back into the mud, dropping the fence post on Allan's hands. He cried out in turn, pulling his hands free.

"Oh!" Jenny cried out, watching both men get injured right in front of her.

———

Lucas had been oiling down his saddle and leather pieces inside the barn when he heard a crash and a piercing gasp. Immediately he dropped his cloth and the reins he'd been working on and ran out to the yard, looking around frantically for what had made those sounds. Even the smallest accident on a ranch could be fatal if not dealt with immediately. He needed to make sure his men were safe, his animals were safe.

He prayed his daughter was inside the house and safe.

As his eyes adjusted to the bright afternoon light, Lucas saw the problem and immediately ran toward the half-repaired fence and the sprawling figures in the mud. The identity of the third person did not register with him immediately; he was not yet used to Miss Sweet being at the ranch at all, let alone expecting to see her with Teddy and Allan outdoors.

"What happened? Are you all right?" he gasped out breathlessly as he reached the site.

Allan sat in the mud with one of the fence rails across his legs as he rubbed a spot just above his right elbow.

"I'm fine," he grumbled. "Might check to see if I got splinters in my palms, but otherwise just a couple bruises." He indicated Teddy with a nod. "Not sure about that one, though."

From where Lucas was standing, Teddy was almost obscured by the figure of Miss Sweet bending over him.

"Miss Sweet? What happened?"

Teddy was groaning in obvious pain as the woman murmured gently to him.

"Miss Sweet?" Lucas said again, more sharply.

She looked up at him in surprise. "One minute."

He was just as shocked by her rudeness as he was by the fact that she was there at all, kneeling in the mud, helping. Whatever he had hoped for or thought he was getting when he hired a housekeeper, this was not it.

After huffing a frustrated breath, Lucas kept quiet; she seemed to be confident in what she was doing and the sooner she could finish the sooner she'd answer him.

"I'm going to need bandages," she said, still in the mud but looking up at Lucas. "And hot water. Could you—"

"Of course. Allan, can you help?"

The other man pulled himself to his feet gingerly. "I'm all right. Just sore. Tell me what to do."

In moments, Allan was running to the ranch house to see if Mrs. Potter was around to heat water, while Lucas ran back to the barn. When his wife was alive, she had stashed a small medical kit just inside the door. Though he wasn't certain what was in it, he could get it to the injured man far more quickly than a trip to the house and back. Speed was key in these situations.

"Here," he said, a bit breathless as he reached Miss Sweet's side. He knelt in the dirt next to her and opened the small wooden case. Inside he found scissors, a tiny bottle of laudanum, a roll of gauze, and a clean towel. "Will this be enough?"

Her eyes passed over the supplies quickly. "For now. We need to get him to the house. I don't trust that any

of those bandages are clean enough for our purposes."
She caught the look on his face. "Sorry."

He shook his head. "Don't be sorry. Just help him."

———

Jenny felt ill.

It wasn't the sight of Teddy's injury, though the fence
rail had crashed into him like a battering ram, breaking a
rib and tearing into his side.

It wasn't the fear or the blood or the danger or even
the nervousness about doing all of this in front of her
new employer.

What was making Jenny feel ill was the memory of
the last time she had tried to help a man with a hole torn
in his side. That scene and the ramifications thereof
were what had driven her from Baltimore, what had
driven her from practicing medicine at all. She'd not
been able to save the man she loved, so what business
did she have trying to help anyone else?

But now, with Teddy groaning and bleeding in front
of her, Jenny knew she could not simply walk away from
him. If she did not take care of this injury now, who
knew what complications would come about before Mr.
Garrett could bring a doctor all the way out here. Teddy
needed her nurse's expertise; this was not a situation she
could run away from.

With shaking hands, Jenny picked up the scissors
from the spare medical kit. She had to put her fear from
her mind, put her past behind her, and give this poor
boy her skill and attention.

Jenny closed her eyes and took a deep breath. When

she opened them again, she got to work cutting the ripped and bloodied shirt off of Teddy's torso. Her hands seemed to be moving on their own, her body remembering all the cuts, bruises, bullet holes, and accidental injuries she had healed in the past. The first thing to do was stop the bleeding, and then she could assess everything and take the first steps to bandaging.

Allan came running back out and, between the three of them, they got Teddy into the house, onto the small cot that stood in Mr. Garrett's office. Mrs. Potter was already heating water and sterilizing more towels for her.

There were a few moments of absolute terror, when Jenny was not certain she could do what needed to be done, but after a long hour of working over the young man, he was soon peacefully resting. A drop of laudanum in tea didn't hurt.

"Thank you, Miss," Teddy said softly as he drifted off to sleep, a wide bandage wrapped around his torso.

CHAPTER FIVE

Teddy's injury had looked bad on first glance, but Jenny was able to stabilize him. Between herself and Mr. Garrett, they got the ranch hand settled, bandaged, and cleaned while Allan went into Juniper Falls for the doctor. He dozed as his body began the slow healing process, and when the doctor arrived that afternoon, Teddy was already insisting that he was fine. Dr. Gilpin gave Jenny further instructions on how to care for the wound, praising what she had already done to aid in the young man's healing.

"This would be a much different conversation if you had not been here, Miss Sweet," he'd said. "This young man is quite lucky."

As she conversed with the doctor, Jenny thought she caught Mr. Garrett watching her carefully, but she kept her focus on the doctor's instructions, trying to put the memories of the man she could not save from her mind. Teddy remained on the cot in the office for the rest of the afternoon, nodding off periodically and joking with her during the few times he was awake, flirting with her, insisting he was fine.

She ignored his claims. Jenny had plenty of experience with patients who cared more about making everyone around them comfortable than about their own healing. Teddy was told in no uncertain terms to stay put, off his feet, while she made supper.

"And then tonight," she said, when she'd followed Mr. Garrett into the office to check on him, "I hope you don't toss and turn too much when you sleep. I'll want to check your bandage first thing in the morning."

"I'll make Allan give me the bottom bunk," Teddy said with a dimpled grin. "No climbing for me for a while, I think."

"You're resting tomorrow, though," she told him.

"Excuse me," Mr. Garrett interrupted coldly. "I don't believe his work duties are up to you."

Jenny swallowed hard, embarrassed that she had spoken out of turn. "You're right. Of course you're right. My apologies. It's just that I used to be—"

"A nurse. Yes, I am aware."

He seemed to glare at her for another long moment before turning to Teddy.

"You should rest tomorrow," he said gruffly.

Jenny ducked her head to hide her smile as she folded one of the blankets at the foot of Teddy's cot to keep her hands busy.

"I've got all that leather you can treat while sitting down," Mr. Garrett continued. "Since I was interrupted in doing that today. Might as well get that done, and I'll help Allan finish the fence."

"Yes, sir."

Jenny brought Teddy a tray of food. After supper, Allan helped him back out to their bunkhouse, Mr. Garrett left to go do something he didn't bother to share, and Mrs. Potter took Mary to get ready for bed, leaving Jenny at the table full of dirty dishes. As she began to clear, she absently thought about when Mary might be old enough to start helping with some of those chores—she'd need to ask Mrs. Potter what she thought. Even working on her own, it didn't take long for Jenny to have the kitchen clean, spick-and-span for the next day.

She was exhausted but satisfied that she'd done good work that day. She tried to hang on to the praise Dr. Gilpin had offered her, keeping her mind from drifting to other things.

She found Mrs. Potter, Mary, and Mr. Garrett in the living room, sitting around the flickering fireplace. The sun had set around suppertime, and the only other light in the room came from an oil lamp on the table next to the older woman. Leaning toward the fire, Mr. Garrett seemed to be whittling something small. Mrs. Potter was reading out loud, while Mary curled up next to her on the settee, her worn doll clutched tightly.

It was a beautiful, homey scene, and Jenny almost felt badly interrupting. Her heart ached a bit, missing her sisters and the cozy nights she had left behind, but this was not her family. If it was not for the fact that it was her duty to see to Mary and get the child to bed, she might have just backed quietly out of the room and not disturbed them.

Though she knew it had only been a few days, Jenny wondered when she would feel as though she were part of this family as well. If ever. When she would feel as though she belonged here. Perhaps she'd be held outside the little circle of affection until her six-month contract was up and she had to start over somewhere else.

But there was just as good of a chance that she'd be the one holding herself back from such intimacy. It was scary. She wasn't sure she was ready to care so much again about another person, even if the Garrett family was amenable.

She drew closer to the tight-knit circle.

"Can I sit?" she asked softly, indicating the empty seat on Mary's other side.

The little girl nodded, and Mrs. Potter did not pause in her reading. Jenny sat quietly, listening, watching, thinking, and enjoying this peaceful moment. When Mrs. Potter reached the end of the chapter, she used a piece of lace as a bookmark and closed the tome.

"That's enough for tonight, young lady," she said as she stood. "My old eyes can't take any more of this. I'm off to bed now, but Miss Sweet will tuck you in later, all right?"

Mary nodded, hopping down off her seat to hug the older woman. "Good night."

Jenny murmured her own goodnight, even as she wondered how she and Mary would spend the next half hour before her bedtime.

"She goes to bed earlier now that you're here," Mary said quietly, watching Mrs. Potter disappear down the dark hallway.

Jenny smiled, certain that the older woman was not going to sleep, but just enjoying the unencumbered time now that she was no longer in charge.

"When I'm a grown-up," Mary continued, "I'm going

to stay up all night. My mama used to let me do that sometimes."

Jenny thought she heard a snort of laughter come from Mr. Garrett, but when she looked up at him, his attention was still on his whittling.

"Did she? How often did that happen?" Jenny asked.

"It happened once," Mr. Garrett interjected, before looking up at his daughter. "And you, miss, were just a little scrap of a thing at the time. How do you remember?"

Mary shrugged.

"New Years Eve," Mr. Garrett continued, for Jenny's benefit. "Mary was three. The last year her mother was alive. And I'm not sure you made it *all* night, but you did stay awake a lot later than we expected."

"Mama said that night was magical. To let the new year in." She scrunched up her face, as though searching for a memory. "Did we open the door, Papa?"

"We did."

"You miss your mother?" Jenny asked quietly.

The little girl nodded.

"I miss my family too."

Mary looked up at her with interest. "Is your family in heaven with Mama?"

Jenny nodded, swallowing down her tears lest she alarm the child. "Some of them, yes. But more of them I left behind in Baltimore. My sisters."

"You have sisters?" Her eyes grew wide.

"I do. Three sisters."

"Wow . . ."

"I bet that seems a little strange to you, doesn't it? Since you've always been the only child."

Mary nodded. "I want a sister. Like Jo March has."

"Have you read that book before?" Jenny asked, remembering exactly what Jo's youngest sister did to her.

Mary shook her head.

"Jo March has three sisters and I have three sisters," Jenny said, deciding not to spoil the story for the little girl. "But I'm the oldest in my family. Then comes Eliza, Abigail, and Beatrice. In fact, now that I think about it, Eliza is an artist just like Jo's sister Amy. That's probably where the similarities end, though."

"When are you going to see your sisters again?"

"I, um . . ." Jenny glanced at Mr. Garrett, who did not seem to be listening. "I'm not sure. It's a long trip back, and I had intended to stay here."

"Maybe they can come visit you."

"Maybe. I just want them to be happy, though, and if staying in Baltimore makes them happy, I'll be all right. We're writing letters."

"If you want, maybe I could write them a letter too. I could tell them to come visit you."

Jenny laughed, appreciating the little girl's generosity. "I love that idea. It's very kind. It's helpful for me to remember that even though my family is far away, they're not gone forever."

"Like Mama," Mary whispered into the top of her doll's head.

Jenny's heart broke to hear the little girl talk so much about the mother she'd barely had time to know. "I'm sorry," she said simply.

Mary looked up at her, eyes shining.

"Sometimes that's all a person can say," Jenny continued. "I'm really sorry that you lost your mother. And I'm sorry that you've had to grow up without her."

Mary looked away again, smashing her face down into the top of the doll's head.

————

Though he wasn't trying to eavesdrop on their conversation, Lucas could not help but overhear Miss Sweet talking to his daughter, asking her about life on the ranch and what she liked about Juniper Falls. In all their correspondence, he'd learned she was a nurse and that she was eager for a fresh start away from Baltimore, though she did not volunteer why. Any questions of her family or other past did not interest him. Those things were not within the scope of her employment. Hearing her talking to Mary, though, Lucas realized how much she had left behind to come here and serve his family. As she continued to ask Mary questions, Lucas found himself sneaking glances at his new housekeeper.

They were discussing the book Mary had been reading with Mrs. Potter, and Miss Sweet's sisters, and then—inevitably—the topic of Mary's mother came up. Lucas clenched his teeth, wishing he had wax or something to stuff in his ears. There wasn't a day that went by that he didn't wish Christine was still alive, if only for Mary's sake, and reminders of her only brought the grief sweeping back in. But that, he supposed, was the very reason he had found Miss Sweet. This smart, capable, and—now he realized—kind and gentle young woman would be as good of a replacement for her mother that he could find.

Though he still resented needing help at all, Lucas found himself surprisingly grateful that Miss Sweet had joined them in Wyoming.

The clock above the fireplace struck eight o'clock.

"Well, my dear," Miss Sweet said as she stood. She held out her hand for Mary to take. "It's about that time. Let's get you ready for bed, and then Papa will come say goodnight to you."

Mary looked at him, her green eyes so like her mother's; Lucas wondered if the day would every go by when he didn't have that thought.

"I'll be right there to tuck you in," he assured her. "Go on with Miss Sweet."

As the two left the warmth of the living room to their bedrooms down the hall, Lucas realized how easily Miss Sweet had fallen into the routine here at his ranch. A good amount of that surely must be due to Mrs. Potter's help and guidance, but he could not deny that Miss Sweet herself made things a lot easier. While her strong opinions and take-charge attitude had irritated him at first, he noticed that she'd quickly learned to hold her tongue most of the time. The exception—when she insisted that Teddy rest and then deferred to Lucas's own authority—was perfectly understandable.

It was far different bringing Miss Sweet into their lives than it had been with Mrs. Potter. The latter had been a friend of the family for years; there had not been any awkward getting-to-know-each-other period. Instead, Mrs. Potter had simply settled into what was now her bedroom and took over the domestic sphere, much to Lucas's relief.

He continued whittling the rook, shaving the small

wood chips into the fire. There was something about Miss Sweet that piqued his curiosity. Perhaps it was simply the way Mary had warmed up to her. He wouldn't have minded listening to her talk about her family and past a bit more.

"Mr. Garrett?"

Lucas looked up to see Miss Sweet in the mouth of the doorway.

"Mary would like you to come say goodnight to her now."

He nodded, stood, and closed the distance between them. His new housekeeper shrunk against the wall when he reached her, giving him as much space to pass as he needed.

He paused before continuing down the hall to his daughter.

"Can I ask you something?" he said quietly.

"Oh!" She seemed surprised. "Yes, I suppose."

"When you were talking to Mary earlier . . . you seemed to imply that you had lost members of your family to more than just your move. Is that true?"

"Um. Yes." She nodded. "My mother passed when I was eighteen. And, um . . ." She cleared her throat and shook her head. "Yes."

"Oh."

She stared at him, as though waiting for him to say more, before filling the silence herself. "Maybe I can be a comfort to Mary in some small way, since I've been through the same thing."

"Maybe."

They looked at each other in the dim light for

another long moment. Lucas cleared his throat awkwardly.

"Well. All right. I suppose I need to go put her to bed."

He continued down the dark hallway toward his daughter's room. The light poured through the door-frame, inviting him into the warmth and comfort that was Mary's presence.

CHAPTER SIX

Jenny was woken out of a deep sleep by the sound of a heavy pounding. It took her a moment to come out of the daze of her dream—something about horses running. The banging pulled at her consciousness until she realized that the heavy knocking was coming from down the hallway. Whatever it was, whoever it was, it sounded urgent. Someone needed attention immediately.

Swiftly, Jenny climbed out of bed, pulled on her wrap, and opened her bedroom door to peer into the hallway. In the couple of weeks since she had arrived at Prairie Winds Ranch, she had yet to experience any similar disturbance; she'd been thrilled at how well she could sleep in this rural environment. Satisfied that the sound was not coming from Mary's room, she slowly made her way to the cold, dark living room. The banging stopped as she noticed a broad-shouldered silhouette reach the front door to the ranch house ahead of her.

The smallest embers still glowed in the fireplace, sending long, dark shadows through the room. Even with no lamp lit, she could tell from the proud, rigid way the silhouette moved that it was Mr. Garrett, coming to see about the banging from his own room on the other side of the house.

With the front door open, Jenny could hear Allan speaking agitatedly, quickly, desperately. Jenny glanced at the grandfather clock next to the hall—one o'clock in the morning. Mr. Garrett said a few words to the ranch hand and closed the door.

"What is it? What's wrong?"

"Storm," Mr. Garrett said shortly. He pulled his heavy coat and scarf from the rack near the door and quickly donned them. As he patted his coat pockets for gloves, a rumble of thunder floated through the walls of the home.

Jenny watched his hurried preparations to head out into the turbulent weather. "Was that Allan?"

He nodded and pulled on his hat.

"Let me get dressed and I'll help," she said.

"There's no need—"

"Don't be silly. Teddy is still recovering, and one of you could get hurt again with the wind blowing like that. I can help. Let me."

He looked at her as he opened the door again. "Just stay out of the way."

Jenny was running back to her room before the front door shut. Her nightdress was far too thin to wear out in that rain and wind, even if she had boots and a coat on over it. Dressing as quickly as she could, her fingers stumbling over the row of tiny buttons up her body,

Jenny mentally made a list of what else she should grab before she ventured into danger. Scissors, perhaps, in case someone got tangled in something. Her own winter gloves, which she had not yet unpacked from her trunk and had to dig out in a hurry. She held a few hair pins loosely between her lips as she walked back down the hallway to the front door.

Hair up. Coat and hat on. Gloves. Boots.

Then out into the storm.

The sound of her gasp was lost to the howling of the wind over the plains. Lightning lit up the yard, followed by a crash of thunder. Immediately she hoped that Mary was able to sleep through this. The ranch house seemed secure enough, and Mrs. Potter was still inside. She trusted them to be fine while she helped the men.

Jenny looked around, wondering where Mr. Garrett had been called to. Wondering where her own assistance might be needed.

The animals in the barn. That would be the place to start.

Squinting against the near-horizontal rain, Jenny plunged into the dark, heading toward where she knew the barn to be. She could feel the mud squelching under her boots, hear the loose boards banging in the wind ahead of her. There was a flash of movement as a lamp was lit inside the barn.

She ran the final steps as lighting zig-zagged across the sky.

The barn doors swung back and forth in the wind with nothing to stabilize them. Where had the boys gone? This could only mean there was worse damage elsewhere. Inside, the sound of the wind was somewhat muted and she heard Mr. Garrett shouting commands. Jenny secured the doors, hoping the break from the wind and rain would make whatever they were attending to easier.

She turned back and took in the scene.

An entire board or two had been ripped off from the top of the building, letting water pour into the hay loft at the far end of the barn. Allan was already up there, moving bales out of the way, hoping to salvage at least some of it from the damp and mold. Teddy was below, shoveling ruined hay to soak up the growing puddles. Though Jenny wanted to admonish him to be careful, she understood that the safety of the animals and securing of the building was far more urgent. Now that she was here, at least, she could take some of the burden. She would just have to check his bandage once this was all over.

Mr. Garrett—in between his shouting—was running all over the place, collecting what he needed to make the necessary repairs as quickly as possible. Ladder, hammer, nails. She watched him yank hard at one of the boards dividing the horse stalls, pulling it off completely to repurpose elsewhere. She winced, thinking about the nails that piece of wood still held, but knew better than to tell the man to be careful.

"You're going up to the roof?" she asked, raising her voice to be heard over the torrents of crashing rain.

"I told you to stay out of the way!" He glared at her, almost dropping the wooden board he held awkwardly with his already-full hands.

"I am! But there's so much— You can't do it all yourself. Especially if you are climbing up to the top of the building in this squall. Let me help!"

"Gotta close up that hole. We can't have this place flooded. What did you think I would do? Just sit on my hands and watch?"

Allan had climbed down from the loft and ran to Mr. Garrett's side. "I'll help. Give me that."

Lightning flashed outside, piercing light coming from the gaps between the boards. Any further conversation was drowned out by the thunder.

But before either man could exit into the torrential storm, another crash from the far end of the barn told them that there was more damage. Jenny looked up in alarm, not just at the sound of the crash, but of the aftermath. The heavy rain falling into the loft had finally broken through, water down dripping through the boards into the horse stalls at the end of the barn.

The animal situated directly under the downpour—a sweet filly named Lacey—panicked at the unexpected change in her usually comfortable home. She backed into the wall, kicking against it with one of her hind legs.

Without thinking, Jenny moved.

She could not climb on top of a barn in the middle of a gale, couldn't rebuild a roof even at the best of times, but she could do this. Keeping the poor animals calm would be something.

"Shhhh, shhh," she began, as she slowly approached the spooked animal.

———

Everything that could go wrong was going wrong, and Lucas was beyond frustrated. A storm was bad enough, but a storm when Teddy was too injured to help? A storm in the middle of the night when all they had was one flickering light and unpredictable lightning to see by? A storm that was loud enough to wake Miss Sweet so now she insisted on being in his way?

He grumbled. Couldn't count on anyone but himself. That was why he'd be the one climbing on top of the barn in all of this.

He'd have to have words with Miss Sweet in the morning, he thought. Make it clear to her where her services were wanted and where she was a nuisance.

But when the rain started pouring in on sweet little Lacey, Lucas felt too defeated to move.

He'd known that the roof of the barn needed to be repaired, but he had hoped that it could last just a few more weeks, just until it got warm enough that he wouldn't have to work in the rain or snow. But he'd waited too long and this final winter storm had finally done it in. Water poured in from above, drenching the loft and the horse stalls underneath.

He was furious with himself by the time he arrived at the barn. It was too much of a risk to light more than one lamp—wind blowing the flame all about—and Lucas struggled through the dim light to even assess what needed to happen. Too much to do. Too few people he could rely on to help. Just like when Christine had died, everything was on him and Lucas did not know how he was going to manage it.

And when Miss Sweet had stumbled through the door, he'd been angry all over again. He had told her to

stay out of the way, but apparently she had not understood that he meant for her to stay in the ranch house.

Now she was halfway across the barn, moving toward
the quickly flooding stalls at the far end where Lacey
was pitching a fit. The filly was already more sensitive
than he liked, but he had been working with her, slowly
training her to be a reliable part of his ranch.

This tumult would undo much of his hard work.

He was torn, frozen in his indecision about whether
to go to calm the horse or to go repair the roof. The
storm did not seem to be abating one inch.

Miss Sweet, however, was proving once again that
she was a steady head in an emergency. He was surprised
into silence, rethinking his earlier frustration.

The former nurse had leapt into action, speaking
calmly and soothingly as she approached the panicked
horse. Before Lucas could even understand what was
happening—this was far from the type of skill he'd
expected of his new housekeeper—Jenny had reached
the nervous filly and was offering her comfort.

He could not believe it. He never would have
thought that a city girl, a nurse for that matter, would
have the gift of soothing a wild creature like Lacey. Not
ever, but certainly not in the middle of a storm like this.
Where he had plunged into a situation assuming the
worst, she was now proving that maybe they could get
through this together.

She turned back to him. Their eyes locked. He
dipped his head a little in a silent thanks.

Offering him a small apologetic smile, Miss Sweet
gestured that he should go out the door, out to the roof.
That she'd stay there with the animals. She had posi-

tioned herself between the horse and the water dripping down, and even from this distance Lucas could see that Miss Sweet's shoulders and back were getting drenched in her efforts to protect the horse.

"Teddy, you stay here and help Miss Sweet. Allan, you come with me."

The two men headed out into the storm, desperately blinking back the rain that slicked down their hats and seeped into their very bones. While repairing a hole in the barn roof was dangerous and difficult in the middle of this storm, knowing that circumstances inside the barn were under control helped Lucas focus and get the job done as quickly as possible.

It seemed that with every day, with every task set in front of her, Jenny Sweet proved more and more that she was indispensable. Lucas could hardly imagine what he would have done this last couple of weeks without her. And that thought worried him. He and Mary had been doing just fine on their own; Mrs. Potter helping out for the last couple of years had done nothing to put a dent in the rigid armor that he kept around his family.

But now this strong woman showed up and, all of a sudden, Lucas was lost without her help.

He didn't want to think about that. He didn't have time to think about that.

As Allan held the ladder steady for him, Lucas climbed carefully, slowly, aware of any potential slip on the wet rungs. It was a gift to have an extra set of hands in the midst of such chaos, and he would just focus on that.

The rain and wind were finally abating when he and Allan climbed down, job done. It had taken a good hour in the storm for them to patch the roof to Lucas's liking. The whole thing would need to be redone on a drier day. But for now, it was taken care of. Lightning and thunder were growing farther apart.

The storm was passing, but for Lucas, this new life settling in with his new housekeeper had just begun.

CHAPTER SEVEN

Jenny's hands were raw after the efforts of the night. She'd stayed calm as much as possible, even while grasping desperately to the reins, the posts, the manes of the horses inside the barn. Helping keep the men safe—and the animals soothed—in the midst of what was the biggest storm Jenny had ever experienced had wrung her out. Even the snow back home was somehow far more mellow and staid than this prairie deluge had been. While she wondered if this was the kind of thing she could look forward to more often, she knew better than to ask Mr. Garrett about it.

He seemed far more shaken up from dealing with the storm than she would have expected. And all of them were exhausted, awake until nearly dawn making repairs, calming the animals, and rebandaging Teddy's injury.

Jenny herself wasn't used to such weather, but she'd expected her employer to be. Instead he seemed frustrated, shaken. As she watched Mr. Garrett put away the hammer, ladder, and other tools, she wished there was something she could do reassure him. He had so much on his shoulders every day; she knew something of that burden and wondered if there were any words of comfort she could offer. She hoped that her assistance, limited though it was, helped at least.

As the sun rose over the hills in the East, she felt proud that she'd found ways to help in a situation that had been so different from what she was used to. Perhaps finding her place would not be as difficult as she'd feared.

If Mr. Garrett let her.

But first, she needed to rest. The ranch hands stumbled to their bunkhouse while Mr. Garrett walked with her back to the home. Jenny felt her whole body relax when she stepped inside the warm living room, even as her boots and coat began dripping on the floor. She was bedraggled, sopping, and too tired to string a whole sentence together.

Mrs. Potter was already up and must have heard them come in. She came bustling into the living room from the kitchen. Jenny took a deep, appreciative sniff, smelling the warm, buttery scent of pancakes.

"You two go to bed," she said, peeling the wet coats off them. "I'll take care of everything today."

Jenny glanced at her employer for his reaction, not wanting to take a day off if he didn't approve of it. He met her eyes, nodded, smiled, and headed off to his own bedroom on the other end of the house. In just a few moments, Jenny had fallen into her own bed, dead to the world.

The next couple of days were blessedly sunny and dry. She was able to sleep through most of that first day, returning to her cooking and child-rearing responsibilities later that afternoon. In the bright midday the next day, the boys had a chance to fix the barn roof properly —Jenny worried the entire time that Teddy was going to hurt himself again—and the muddy puddles became packed dirt. On the third day of such sun, she thought it would be a good chance to get some work done outdoors before the spring rainstorms found them.

"I think it's about that time," Jenny said excitedly as she cleared the dishes after breakfast. She had gone out to get water earlier that morning and taken the opportunity to look around.

"What time?" Mary looked up from her fried potatoes with guarded interest.

"The frost is just about gone and it's time to start our vegetable garden. Would you like to help me?"

"Oh, yes please!" The little girl lit up.

"Perfect. I know you'll be a big help. Let's get the kitchen clean, and then we'll start."

Mary beamed under her encouragement, and Jenny felt herself put down one more tiny root here. She could not help but adore this sweet, motherless child, though she was not brave enough to look ahead to September and what might be waiting for her if Mr. Garrett didn't want to extend her contract.

After breakfast, after the dishes were washed and put away, Jenny got Mary dressed for the outdoors. Coat. Hat. The little girl could not find her gloves at first, but Mrs. Potter helped. And then the pair marched purposefully outside, ready for the spring season to begin in earnest.

Some twenty yards or so from the house, the

remnants of last year's garden were still identifiable; Jenny could see the borders of the plot clearly in the sunniest part of the yard. Given that the ranch had an extra person this year, she planned on expanding the plot by a few feet, but otherwise the process of getting the ground turned over, weeded, and seeds sown would not be terribly difficult.

"All right, Miss Garrett," Jenny began authoritatively, handing the little girl her pair of gloves. "Would you prefer to help pull up weeds with me or to walk the length of the garden to move any stones and other debris that has found its way in over the winter?"

"What's deb— Debris?"

"Oh, sometimes it's garbage or sticks or really anything that doesn't belong. Once, back home, we didn't clear our garden thoroughly before the spring and squirrels came looking for the nuts they'd buried. We had to plant the whole thing over again."

Jenny had knelt at the edge of the plot and pulled on her own gloves.

"Who did you have a garden with?" Mary asked as she knelt next to Jenny. The little girl still had not let go of her doll, setting the stuffed toy in her lap. She watched for a moment, before leaning forward to pull up the grass that had begun to grow, copying Jenny as closely as possible with one hand.

"My sisters and my parents."

"You have three sisters, like in *Little Women*, right?"

"That's right. The garden was for six people, but it wasn't very big. There was only room for a couple of our favorite vegetables. We lived in a row house in a city, so we only had a tiny patch behind the house. But there were squirrels everywhere and they didn't have many other places to store their nuts."

"What about your husband?"

Jenny felt herself go cold all over, but forced her voice to remain somewhat level. "What do you mean, pet?"

"You're so pretty and nice. You have a husband, don't you?"

"Oh . . ." Jenny thought fast, trying to both catch up to what this child believed of married life and figure out how to steer her correctly. "No, I don't have a husband. Not everyone gets married. And some people have husbands and wives that . . . that are in heaven."

"Like Papa."

"Exactly like your papa. We know that he's sad, because your mother is gone, but we also know he's still good and strong and reliable, don't we?"

"Yes. Like you're still pretty even though you don't have a husband to tell you so."

Jenny laughed. "Exactly like that."

A shadow crossed the dirt in front of her, and Jenny looked up to see her employer standing at the edge of the garden plot. She wasn't sure how long he'd been standing there, how much he had heard. But given the potential for misunderstanding and what she'd interpreted to be his frustration the night of the storm, she wondered if, perhaps, a moment for just the two of them might be warranted.

"Mary, honey, would you go inside for me and get the seeds? They're in a brown envelope in the basket by the cellar door. Bring it right back out here, please."

The little girl nodded somberly and ran to obey, still clutching her doll tightly.

Once she was gone, Jenny looked up into Mr. Garrett's face, backlit by the sun high in the sky.

"Hello," she said simply, waiting for whatever judgment or scolding he might have for her.

———

Lucas watched his little girl run into the house and realized he had been left alone with Miss Sweet. Though he wouldn't say that he had been deliberately avoiding her, neither was he seeking out opportunities like this to speak to her. Somehow, he felt if they spent too much time together, he would find himself vulnerable. He was not ready for that.

"You don't need seeds yet," he pointed out, unable to keep the confusion from his voice. "You've barely started weeding. I know you're a city girl, but I would have thought Mrs. Potter would have explained. We need one of the boys to turn over the earth for you first."

"No, you're right," she said frankly, "but I did need a moment alone with you and it is good for Mary to feel like she's needed."

Lucas frowned. This was not why he'd interrupted his own work to come over here. "What did you need to talk to me alone about?"

Miss Sweet looked back over her shoulder quickly, checking for his daughter. "I wonder if you have time today to help us with the vegetable garden. I know—" She held up her hand to forestall his protests, and he shut his mouth sullenly. "I know perfectly well that I can do this all on my own, but I think it would be good for Mary to see you working alongside her. For the two of you to complete a project together."

"She sees me do things around the ranch every single day."

"But she's not doing it *with* you. She misses her mother, of course, and I don't think you want her missing her father when you're just on the other side of the ranch."

"Hmm."

"I really don't mean to overstep. But I know what it's like to lose a parent. She's plenty old enough to learn how a working farm operates, and to see you investing your energy and strength into her home would do her some good. The reminder that she still has that stability and home even without her mother could be monumental."

"But . . . now? Can't there be something else? I still need to repair the barn stalls as soon as possible."

"Well, it's your choice, of course," Miss Sweet said, deferring to his authority. "But the vegetable garden also needs to be put in soon, and this seems like the kind of project that a five-year-old could be great at. Digging in the soil? Moving rocks around? I can't imagine you want her at your side when you're castrating a bull, for example."

"Well, no," he admitted.

"She'll be going to school in the fall, won't she? This may be the last time you truly have her home with you, and at this age what she needs most is—"

"Her mother," he interjected.

"No. That's not what I was going to say." She paused,

watching him. Her expression softened. "What Mary needs most is a parent. Someone who she knows is not going anywhere, who she knows she can count on. In five, ten years, when she's grown and makes a mistake or has trouble, don't you want to be the person she thinks to come to? That kind of trust and safety starts now. When she's five."

"She has that."

"Of course *I know* she has that, but she still needs you to *show* her that. That's how she learns it to be true."

Lucas fell silent. The last thing he needed was to be lectured on how to be a better parent by this woman who had only just shown up. He could acknowledge—grudgingly—that she was not completely without experience. Helping to raise her three younger sisters after her mother's death could not have been easy. But Miss Sweet did not know him. Did not yet know his daughter.

"I'll . . . I need to think about it."

She nodded, understanding. "Of course. It's something we can fortunately revisit every day. As long as Mary is growing up, she'll need you. If you don't want to work on the garden with us today, maybe tomorrow."

She shrugged and returned her focus to clearing the dirt in front of her. Mary emerged from the house then and ran toward her.

"I found them!" she shouted, running on her chubby legs. She still clutched her doll in one arm and held the envelope of seeds in the other. "Papa, are you going to help us?"

"Um . . ."

He looked at Miss Sweet who, to her credit, remained passive and did not seem to be trying to sway him one way or another. He looked back to his daughter who was all but jumping up and down in anticipation.

"I can stay for a little bit. Allan and I need to get the repairs in the barn finished soon, but I also want to see how you are helping Miss Sweet. All right?"

"Yes!" she exclaimed happily. "Which seeds do you want?"

Mary set her doll down in the dirt at her feet. Lucas almost said something to her about taking care of her things, but realized that if she could let go of the toy that had brought her such comfort, then the alternative —working alongside her father—must be offering her even more.

He softened as he saw the way his precious daughter was blossoming under the careful guidance of Miss Sweet.

Looking up at him with adoration, Mary held out her palm under the sealed envelope, as though getting ready to dump the entire collection.

"Not yet, dear," Miss Sweet said, closing her hands over Mary's own. "We're still weeding and moving the rocks and things. That's why we need your papa's help."

"Because he's strong, right?"

Miss Sweet glanced at Lucas, blushing prettily before answering Mary's question. "He's very strong, yes, and so are you. Strong and smart and I know that between the three of us we can get this whole lot cleared before your papa needs to go back to help Allan, right?"

"Okay."

CHAPTER EIGHT

Jenny yawned, stretching her arms over her head before sinking even more cozily into the settee. Mary had just been put to bed, Mrs. Potter had retired earlier, and now she and Mr. Garrett sat in comfortable silence in the big living room. A fire crackled in the hearth, creating a warm, cozy bubble against the cold outside. Even with the days warming, the nights remained chilly. Jenny was grateful for the quilt spread over her knees as she curled up with her cup of tea and needlepoint.

It had been a long day of clearing space for the garden—satisfying, but she was still tired. Working alongside Mary and Mr. Garrett had been enlightening, and she found herself with a better understanding of the hard exterior he showed the world. It was clear from just those few hours that he treasured Mary beyond anything else on this earth. She looked at him now, across the living room, and felt a small stirring of affection for the man protecting his wounded heart while trying to give his daughter everything.

If all she did during these six months of her contract was help those two build a stronger bond, she would be satisfied.

She stretched again. After several hours of clearing weeds and stones, her arms and shoulders were tired and sore. She had thought being a nurse was physically demanding, but that was nothing compared to what keeping house for a rancher and taking care of a child required of her. She was doing her best to not ask Mrs. Potter for too much; the older woman deserved whatever rest she could get. Over the several weeks that she'd been at Prairie Winds Ranch, Jenny had learned so much, tried so many new things, and discovered reserves in her that had not been called upon in her career as a nurse.

But despite how busy she had been kept, Jenny could not quite forget what she'd left behind in Baltimore, nor could she shake the feeling of terror and uncertainty that had overwhelmed her when Teddy had been hurt. Even though she had been a nurse for years, had helped hundreds if not thousands of people, had seen all manner of illness and injury, there was one patient who she could not get out of her mind. That man who she would have done anything for, and yet, when it came to it, she could do nothing for.

It was the memory that she had hoped to blot out by moving to the other side of the continent.

Her needlepoint fell, untouched, in her lap as she thought back to that harrowing experience.

The year before, about this time in late winter, Jenny had been walking through the narrow streets of Baltimore on her way to the hospital with her fiancé, David Watts, at her side. She and Dr. Watts had met years earlier working at the hospital. They had built a firm friendship based on mutual respect and a love for helping others before David had even hinted that he might like to court her. She adored him and could not wait to spend every day with him, counting herself lucky with every one of their hospital shifts that overlapped. He had proposed at Christmas and they were planning a summer wedding.

But even with these big changes to their relationship and to their future plans, Jenny and David still met to walk to work every day. It was a quiet, simple routine that formed the foundation of her life. She did not know what she would do without that steady rhythm, and she certainly did not know what she would do without David. They had already agreed that she would continue to work after they wed, at least for a little while.

That particular day in late March, David had been telling her excitedly about the advancements that were being made in surgical treatments. One of the things she'd enjoyed so much about him was how deeply he loved his work. He loved his patients. He would work tirelessly to help them, writing to other experts all over the world if necessary to ask questions and learn more. Some days he only stopped to eat lunch because the mothers of the boys whose broken limbs he'd set or the wives of the men who had been treated for irregular heartbeats came all the way to the hospital to bring him a sandwich or a fresh piece of fruit from their gardens.

Dr. David Watts was Jenny's favorite person, and on

that morning, as they walked together to the hospital to begin their workday, she reflected how grateful she was to have met him at all. He held her gloved hand tightly as they turned down the wide street that would lead them to the hospital.

They'd heard a scream of terror echoing off the buildings, but before Jenny could even turn to see what was wrong, David's hand was violently yanked from her own as she was shoved to the side of the street. She stumbled over her feet, knocking her shoulder into the brick building hard. When she regained her balance and looked up, David was gone. After a brief moment of confusion, Jenny panicked.

She spotted—

She wanted to be wrong and tried not to panic. After years of experience working as a nurse, calming patients with injuries and illnesses, she would have hoped she'd be able to handle this better.

But she had spotted a block down what appeared to be a crumpled body, discarded on the side of the street. There was a crowd quickly growing around it, and a carriage with two spooked horses was being brought under control just past the scene of the disaster.

Jenny's stomach dropped. She thought she was going to be sick, but then she did what any doctor or nurse would do.

She ran to help.

When she reached the injured person, she froze, taking in the sight.

David must have pushed Jenny out of the way as his very last act before the horses had run him down. There was so much blood, she could not be certain where it was coming from. There were too many injuries, she didn't know where to start. Truly, it was only because she knew him, knew his attire so intimately, that she was able to identify him as Dr. David Watts at all. His legs were both broken, bent in unnatural positions. One arm was flung straight up from his shoulder, while the other rested across his chest. Several bones in his face had been crushed.

But the worst—the immediate life-threatening injury —was the gaping hole in David's side, just at the bottom of his rib cage. Even through the layers of clothing and the blood, Jenny thought she could spot a broken bone. Perhaps one of the horses had kicked out at him with their strong hooves in the panic to get away; perhaps a bit of a nearby cart or carriage had impaled him as he was dragged past. Whatever the cause, the result was blood pouring from him as he lay unconscious.

Jenny swallowed hard, feeling as though she might throw up, but she pushed all that fear and heartbreak down and stepped into action. She ran to David's side to do everything she knew how to do. Peeling back the clothes as carefully as she could. Calling for scarves or coats or blankets from the crowd gathering. She had to focus. She had to prioritize this if she was going to be able to save him.

His blood was all over her hands; when she pushed loose hair out of her face, she felt it streak across her forehead.

But she didn't care. She didn't stop to clean any of it. The only thing she cared about was stopping the bleeding.

Saving his life.

Another bystander had joined her by then, and they worked shoulder-to-shoulder to try to hold the injured man together. To staunch the outpour. Someone had handed over a shawl, now folded up and held against the wound. Someone else was keeping the crowd back to give Jenny room to work.

But all of it was in vain.

Jenny saw immediately that this was not an injury anyone could come back from, but she didn't want to believe it. He was so strong; surely she could find the right combination of treatments to convince his body to hold on to life.

She didn't even realize she was crying until she noticed a tear dropping from the tip of her nose to the bloodied sleeve of her dress.

She had no idea how long she knelt there trying to help him. They'd had to pry her away from his dead body, bleeding out in the street, and Jenny remembered very little of what happened over the following weeks. She held a vague memory of helping David's mother make funeral plans, and another foggy recollection of wandering around the home she shared with her sisters in a stunned stupor. But when the graphic, bloody image of David flashed through her mind, she flinched. Closed her eyes. Tried to push it out.

Now, here in Wyoming, it all came flooding back. She shivered despite the warmth of the fire and pulled her quilt higher around her. Jenny wondered if the day would ever come that she was not shaken by the memory. It was truly the only difficult moment she and David had ever shared, but it was monumental. While she was grateful for the comfort of his memory in every other way, she wished she could forget that final moment.

The whole reason she had packed up her entire life, after all, was to put that memory from her mind. She'd hoped that a new home, new friends, entirely new landscape would give her a new view on life, but instead it seemed as though everything still reminded her of that traumatic moment and what she'd lost. Tending to Teddy's wound the week before had only reminded her of a similar heart-wrenching final moment with David.

After taking a long leave of absence from the hospital, Jenny found she could not bring herself to return to the place where they'd met. Where they'd fallen in love. Where so many of her most treasured memories of him occurred. Instead of returning to her occupation as a nurse, she'd looked for escape, and that was when she'd found and responded to Mr. Garrett's employment offer nearly two thousand miles away.

Even after all that effort, the memories had found her anyway.

She sighed heavily.

———

That sigh sounded far more distraught than Lucas would have expected from his new housekeeper. She'd been cheerful and steady over the weeks she'd been there, and he'd seen nary a hint of a cloud in her demeanor. But now, he realized she'd been sitting watching the fire for several minutes, looking more and more dejected.

He cleared his throat. He wasn't sure what to say, how to comfort her, though it was clear that Miss Sweet was sad over something. He searched back in his memories of what he knew had happened that day and concluded that perhaps this was just one of the many mysteries that existed when living side by side with a woman. He trusted that if she wanted to talk about her troubles, she would.

It dismayed him some to realize that he may not be the person she would choose to open her confidences to. And that dismay surprised him. He had so withdrawn from even friendship over the last couple of years that he did not feel prepared for this.

While Mrs. Potter had taken care of his home over the years since his wife had died, somehow her presence had not prepared him for that of Miss Sweet. Perhaps it was that Miss Sweet worked harder to be part of Mary's life, or that she was still learning how the ranch worked and so asked more questions. Whatever it was, Lucas found himself noticing Miss Sweet every day far more than he had the older woman.

And now that she was sitting, quietly weeping across the room from him, he felt a subtle desire to comfort her. To fix whatever was wrong.

Lost in his thoughts, he must have stopped whittling long enough for her to notice. She looked up at him, their eyes meeting across the living room, the firelight sending flickering shadows between them.

"I'm sorry," she said. She brushed away a tear and offered him a brave smile. "I don't mean to disturb you."

"You're not." His voice was soft, concerned. "Are you . . . Would you like to talk about it?"

She shook her head. Then nodded. Then laughed at herself. "I don't know."

"All right."

They sat awkwardly in silence for several moments before she cleared her throat. "When we were corresponding, when I was applying for this job, did I happen to mention why I wanted to get out of Baltimore?"

He thought back, chagrined to realize he had no recollection of even asking her, let alone getting an answer to that somewhat important question. He should have shown more interest. He could have been a better friend to this woman who was picking up her whole life to come help him. Embarrassed, he shrugged.

"I, um . . . No. I don't think so."

She nodded, thinking. "It's far in the past now, and I have grieved and healed—or so I thought. It's just that everything that happened with Teddy brought it all up again, reminding me of my own limitations, and I . . . I just worry that I'm going to let you down. Let Mary down. I came all this way for a fresh start, but then . . . I couldn't run away from myself, I suppose."

"I suppose not."

Lucas looked down at his hands, at the wedge of soft wood that he was whittling into another rook for the chess set he was making so he could teach Mary. It wasn't important right now; her feelings were. But he didn't know quite what to say, what she might need.

He cleared his throat. "I'm sorry," he said again.

She offered him a brave smile, but did not volunteer any more. As she picked up her needlepoint again, Lucas found himself hoping that she would feel at home here soon. Whatever she had left in Baltimore was still there;

between himself and Mary, perhaps they could help Miss Sweet settle into Wyoming.

He found himself hoping she would consider the Prairie Winds Ranch her home and was grateful that she had no intention to return to her home in the East.

CHAPTER NINE

"All right, then, Teddy," Jenny said as she leaned back into her chair. She had been replacing the dressing over his wound and checking the progress. "The wound is healing to my liking, but you're the only one who can say how deep the bruising goes. If you can take a deep breath without pain, then I suppose there's no more reason for me to keep you off your feet."

She and the ranch hand were seated on the front porch in the cool morning air while Jenny gave him a final check-up. Though Teddy had been cheerful and joking about his time as an invalid, it was apparent to everyone how much he wanted to be moving again. Climbing, running, laughing. He seemed to be in perpetual motion; being asked to be careful and stay still had been anathema to Teddy, but Jenny had insisted as kindly as she could.

As she spoke, he grinned and took a comically deep, performative breath, shoulders rising almost to his ears to demonstrate just how much he could do without pain.

"You know if you push yourself before you're ready, it'll just mean more rest, don't you?" Jenny teased. "You wouldn't lie to me about how you're feeling just so you can go into town with Allan, would you?"

"No, ma'am," Teddy said, standing. "I really do feel completely better."

"It's probably not *completely* better, but I think it's enough. And you'll tell me if you have pain again?" Everything indicated to Jenny that the broken rib was essentially healed, and all of her past experiences with injured young men told her that there was no point in admonishing him further. He was going to do what he was going to do regardless of her guidance.

He nodded, already halfway to the steps leading off the porch.

"Go on then," she said indulgently. "I'll see you at supper. Have fun in town."

She watched as he ran across the yard to where Allan was waiting with the wagon. The two boys were driving into Juniper Falls that day to have a meal at the Sunshine Cafe and to collect the mail and other supplies that Mr. Garrett had ordered a few weeks earlier. Jenny had to admit being a little bit envious of their plans; she would have liked to be around more people, meet some of her neighbors and—if she was honest—eat a meal that someone else had prepared.

The ranch would be quiet without them, and as they drove off, Jenny knew she would have plenty to fill her day here.

The front door opened and Mary stepped out onto the porch next to her, clutching her doll tightly to her face. After yesterday afternoon, when Jenny had been able to get the little girl working side by side with her father, she'd not seen the doll at all. Its reappearance as Mary's security comfort meant nothing good.

"You finished your breakfast?" Jenny asked. "And took your dirty dishes into the kitchen?"

Mary nodded, looking past Jenny to the bare yard. She sniffed. "What are you doing?"

"I was just checking on Teddy before they left. What are you doing?"

The little girl shrugged and buried her face in the doll's hair, sniffing again.

"You feeling all right?" Jenny asked softly.

"I think my doll is sick maybe," Mary murmured.

Jenny smiled to herself, recognizing the same trick her younger sister Eliza used to play. When she could not bear to be left out of things, but was too tired or too ill to participate, she blamed any reticence on—in Eliza's case—a pet. It seemed as though Mary's doll offered the same protection.

"Oh, well then, we must make sure your doll rests so she's not sick any longer than necessary. Should we go put her to bed? Maybe fill a hot water bottle for her?"

Mary looked up at Jenny with her big green eyes and nodded. "She doesn't want to be sick tonight when the boys come back from town with treats."

"Very smart." Jenny nodded seriously. "Let's take care of her."

Once Mary was tucked into bed with a hot water bottle and starting to nod off, Jenny checked in with Mrs. Potter and then headed to the ranch yard to look for Mr. Garrett. Though Jenny had plenty to do, she would let him know about Mary first. Perhaps with the two ranch hands gone for most of the day, he needed assistance himself.

As she walked toward the barn, Jenny looked at the fields stretching to the horizon. With almost ten thousand acres, the herd of cattle had so much space to roam that she only saw them every other day or so, when Teddy and Allan drove them to graze nearer to the house. There was a rhythm to life out here that she was just starting to sense, especially with the first notes of spring weather. It was far different than her life in the city, going to the hospital every day rain or shine, early sunset or late. There had been days in the winter when she'd be indoors from dawn until dusk, but here she'd seen Mr. Garrett change his plans for the day simply based on whether or not the mud had dried after rain from the day before.

It was fascinating to Jenny; she realized that if she could just slip into the rhythm of the seasons here, it may go a long way toward helping her put her grief and pain behind her.

When she didn't see Mr. Garrett anywhere outside, Jenny thought she'd check inside the barn. She couldn't think where else he might be on his own. Fortunately, her searching ended when she walked inside. She found him carrying several wooden boards and called out.

"Mr. Garrett? Do you need any help with that?"

He paused in his steps and turned toward her voice. Then he looked past her and frowned.

"Where's Mary?"

"She was a bit sniffly this morning, so I've put her to bed. I'm sure she'll be fine, but resting is always a safe bet. Mrs. Potter is knitting in the living room, so she'll hear if Mary calls out or needs something. She told me she wanted to be well tonight when the boys come back from town."

Mr. Garrett grinned. "That girl. She knows that they always bring her a treat of some kind. She has those boys wrapped around her finger."

"Well then I, too, am excited to see what they bring back." She grinned in return. "So, anyway, if you need another set of hands, I have a little time."

He nodded. "All right. Then . . . Yes, if you're offering to help and there's nothing in the house that requires your attention this moment, I'd appreciate it."

"Of course."

She beamed at him, unexpectedly thrilled for this chance to spend time with him. She told herself it was the opportunity get to know her employer better and learn more about how the ranch worked that excited her. With every day it seemed as though she was putting down more roots, finding herself more firmly in this new life.

———

Lucas had spent nearly half an hour that morning alone at the huge, old bur oak tree just a little past the barn. It was one of his favorite places on the ranch, and the place he went when he needed to think. He didn't know quite how old the tree was, but just being in its presence helped remind him how small his immediate, earthly concerns were compared to the whole of time. He always walked away from those brief communes with at least a little clarity.

His own tenderness toward Miss Sweet the night before had shocked him, and those thoughts had kept him awake later than he'd like. This morning, after a few moments of quiet reflection, he realized that there was something about her that reminded him of himself. He had spent the last two years ignoring his own thoughts and feelings, focusing on Mary and the ranch, and it seemed as though Miss Sweet was heading down the same road.

He did not know what he needed, nor what she might need. He could only look to the step immediately in front of him, but at least he could offer her grace and understanding.

Now, as he accepted her help with his repairs, Lucas wondered if she, too, used work to distract herself from her feelings. He didn't expect his new housekeeper to be quite so eager to do more labor around the ranch. He'd set his expectations low, telling himself that she'd agreed to only a six-month contract for a reason. If Mary stayed safe and the boys stayed fed, he didn't ask for much else and would deal with replacing her when the time came.

But here she was, happy to add even more to her day on top of caring for a sick child and all the other tasks she had to worry about.

Though Lucas wouldn't say so to Miss Sweet, he was grateful she'd come to offer him help. He would have been able to finish the repairs on his own, eventually, with effort and risk of injury, but with her steady hands next to him it would go much more quickly.

"Where do you want me to start?" she asked, looking around the barn.

"Let me just let the horses into the paddock," he

said, "and then we'll have all the space we need. We're going to rebuild the walls of the stalls."

As he was leading Lacey, Bo, and Flibbit out through the wide, open doors, Lucas noticed Miss Sweet pull a heavy pair of gloves out of the pocket of her coat. He couldn't help but admire a woman who always seemed prepared. When he returned to the stall where the boards were missing, she was kicking aside some of the hay in the bottom of the stall to give them a flat surface to stand on.

"I'd like you to hold the new boards in place for me, and I'll take care of nailing them in." He pointed to where a stack of fresh lumber sat to the side. "I just finished cutting these pieces down, so we should be able to move quickly."

She nodded briskly, alert and focused on the task at hand; Lucas could easily imagine how efficient a nurse she must have been, silently taking instructions and handling every detail. As he watched, she confidently picked up one of the boards—longer than she was tall— and carried it to the spot he had indicated. The wood that had been damaged in the storm or repurposed that night for repairs all needed to be replaced now. There were a few boards here, a few there, including one that cracked when the filly Lacey had panicked and kicked at it.

They worked side by side in silence for almost half an hour. Though he kept thinking of questions he wanted to ask her, Lucas held his tongue. The quiet wasn't awkward, and he was wary of being overly personal with her. He had, after all, told Miss Sweet on the day that she arrived that she was not here to be anyone's friend;

he could not very well try to change that now even if he was interested in hearing about her life in Baltimore.

Even if he was interested in hearing about what had made her sigh so despondently the night before.

For her part, Miss Sweet seemed eager to learn about what was needed to keep the ranch working. She asked questions when she had them, and he had never needed to repeat himself. He was surprised how well she could follow even his more complicated instructions.

"Head's up!" Lucas called, just before he tossed the board to Miss Sweet.

Her reflexes were deft and she had no trouble clutching the wooden plank out of the air when it reached her. She laughed in delight at her own skill, her eyes sparkling as they met his.

"Nice work," he said approvingly.

She was more nimble at that than Christine had been.

He caught himself in a feeling of betrayal—his wife had only ever done her best. She was never terribly healthy after they moved to the frontier. That first winter in Wyoming, Christine had caught pneumonia and her health was never the same. And then after Mary was born, Christine just got weaker and weaker until finally she'd passed one late winter two years prior. When the snow began to melt and the ground began to thaw, Lucas was unfailingly reminded of his wife's death.

It was those very memories that he was trying to distract himself from now, keeping himself busy with tasks that could have waited until the ranch hands had returned.

But doing this work with Miss Sweet at his side had

reminded Lucas of how good it could be to have a help-mate, to not feel as though everything was on his shoulders alone.

He wondered if he could make her laugh like that again.

"Maybe don't toss me anything bigger than this though," she said over her shoulder with a teasing grin. "I'm used to much smaller things like bandages and vials of medicine."

He didn't want their afternoon together to end. As he watched her situate the board in place, Lucas racked his brain for another task they could take on together, another chance to work toward a goal side by side.

CHAPTER TEN

With Teddy and Allan in town for the day, Jenny had just finished helping her employer repair the boards that made up the horse stalls in the barn. She'd been surprised that he would have been able to do all of that on his own, given that the boards were more than six feet long. Though they'd worked in silence, she'd spent the time wishing she could ask questions—about Mary, about his past, about how he ended up with this ranch—but he'd been so prickly and distant since she'd arrived that she knew better than to press in any way.

In the few weeks she'd been living on the ranch, she'd known Mr. Garrett as a stoic, distant man. He was never rude to her, but he certainly lacked the warmth and welcome that would have helped make this ranch a home for Jenny. It was apparent that he treasured his daughter and wanted the best for her, but for the most part he held himself at arm's length from everyone else who lived at the ranch. As he finished putting away the hammer and nails from their construction project, the bright daylight poured into the barn from the open doors. Jenny noticed a thoughtfulness in his expression, but he kept whatever he was thinking to himself.

When she'd been working as a nurse, she'd had her share of patients who didn't want anything to do with her, who didn't want to say a word or explain themselves or be told what to do, even as they nursed a wound or illness. Mr. Garrett reminded her of those patients somehow. Though he had not mentioned his wife or his life before Jenny had gotten there, it was clear from his standoffishness and silence on the subject that he guarded that wound viciously.

Not that she could blame him for that.

She wouldn't force any disclosure he did not want to give, even if she was curious.

She didn't want to be too involved anyway, Jenny reminded herself. It was enough that this man had given her a way to escape Baltimore. Anything more than that might get too close to her own heartbreak that she was still carefully healing.

He closed his toolbox and Jenny shook herself out of her thoughts. It was time to look forward, not back. With the barn repairs completed, she had the whole afternoon ahead of her. There was always laundry to do, and baking, and she wanted to scrub the living room floor. She wondered if she would have time to write a letter to her sisters before she needed to start supper.

"I appreciate your help," Mr. Garret said, interrupting her planning. "I wonder if I might offer my help in return with one of your own projects."

That surprised her, and Jenny looked up at his hesitant expression in wonder. He seemed almost embarrassed to be volunteering a thought at all, let alone assistance. Jenny thought she'd noticed a bit of gruffness to his voice that hadn't been there before.

"I'm not doing laundry," he clarified gruffly. "I had something else in mind."

Jenny couldn't help but laugh at that, picturing tall, ruggedly handsome Mr. Garrett with his sleeves rolled up so he could scrub at grass stains against a washboard.

"All right. Can't say I blame you," she answered with a grin. "What did you have in mind? I'm happy to get to whatever needs doing on your ranch."

"Since the boys are gone," Mr. Garrett offered, "why don't I help you turnover the soil for the garden? We don't want that delayed any longer than necessary. If we get the seeds in soon enough, and if we're lucky with the weather, we might even have enough time for a second late summer planting."

"Really?" Jenny lit up. "That would be— Thank you, yes. I would love to get the garden started. Especially the hardest part that Mary can't really help with."

He nodded before looking around the barn's interior. "All right. I see the two shovels here, but let me also go get the hoe . . . I think it's outside the boys' bunkhouse. Why don't you take one of those and I'll meet you at the vegetable patch in five minutes?"

"The day is getting warmer. I'll grab us canteens, too," she called over her shoulder as she headed toward the house, shovel in hand.

This was certainly not how she expected to be spending her day. Though she wondered how Teddy and Allan were enjoying their time in Juniper Falls, Jenny found herself perfectly happy to be at Prairie Winds

Ranch on this beautiful spring day. That indefinable scent of growing things was in the air; even in the city she'd noticed how things shifted in the spring. She was thrilled that Mr. Garrett had offered to help her till the soil that afternoon. Jenny had a sneaking suspicion that she could very easily fall in love with gardening.

Mrs. Potter was still knitting in the living room when Jenny entered. She was assured that Mary was just fine, resting and playing quietly in her room. The older woman only nodded in response when Jenny told her she'd be outside for much of the afternoon. Once in the kitchen, she washed her hands and looked around for some other treat she could bring Mr. Garrett. He worked so hard every day to provide not just for his daughter but also for the other four people living on the ranch. If there was a tiny bit of joy or sustenance she could offer him, she wanted to.

Plus, she was hungry herself from working harder that morning than she was used to. She was getting more comfortable with living on a ranch, and looked forward to the coming warmer season when they would be able to spend more and more time outdoors, the sun setting later each evening.

There was a little bit of leftover breakfast—biscuits and jam. Even the small amount would be better than nothing and keep them sated for a while longer while they worked. Quickly, Jenny slathered fresh butter and strawberry preserves on the cold biscuits before wrapping them up in a towel and tying the whole package closed. The canteens hung by the kitchen door, mostly full, so she looped them over her shoulder on her way out into the sunshine.

Mr. Garrett stood at one end of the plot of dirt that Jenny and Mary had spent hours clearing of stones, weeds, and other debris that had settled in over the winter. The ground was still hard and packed, though not frozen, and their task today would be to till the earth.

She paused, watching him work for a moment before joining him. His strong arms strained against the several layers of clothing he wore as he struggled to dig into the compacted earth, heavy with months of winter weather.

"I brought you a bite to eat," she called as she approached.

Mr. Garrett looked up, surprised. "Oh— Thank you. That's thoughtful."

"I figured I'm hungry so you might be too." She offered him a smile while she untied the towel-wrapped biscuits and withdrew one for herself. "I can bring you soap and water if you want to wash your hands—"

"No need." He took his own biscuit with murmured thanks. "My mama used to say that we all have to eat a peck of dirt before we die."

Jenny laughed hesitatingly, unsure if he was serious. "Um, I uh . . . I'm not sure that's what that saying means."

She noticed the twinkle in his eye as he grinned at her over his food.

"Oh, you're teasing me," she said with a relieved chuckle. "Well, speaking as a medical professional, I'm sure you'll be just fine."

"Thank you, nurse."

Jenny warmed under his smile, realizing that this day was the first time they'd spent alone since the very first drive from the train station. It also was practically the first time she'd heard him joking and light-hearted. Her first impression of him was very different from this man standing in front of her. That first drive from Laramie had been a very different experience, overwhelmed as she'd been by all the new sights and sounds and smells and people.

Suddenly she felt self-conscious, aware of all this time to get to know him better as he seemed to be warming to her. She took a bite of her own biscuit, turning away from her employer and looking out over the yard toward the main road that passed the ranch.

"I don't know how a person could ever get used to a view like this, so much beauty in every direction," she said, looking out over the first hints of meadow coming up. Far in the distance were tall mountains, the tallest peaks still snow-capped. "Back East, the only direction you could see even half this far was toward the ocean. My fiancé took me sailing once and—"

Jenny stopped, heart pounding as she realized that she had just broken her promise to herself to not look back, to not mention or even think about her life with David if she could help it. She was glad her back was to Mr. Garrett, as she was terribly afraid she was going to cry. Taking a big bite of biscuit, Jenny tried to put her loss from her mind, focusing on the immediate project right in front of her.

After a long moment of silence, she heard Mr. Garrett's tentative question.

As he ate the biscuit and jam that she'd brought, Lucas waited for Miss Sweet to continue. Her silence made him worry about her; she seemed perturbed simply by mentioning her fiancé. He realized suddenly, watching the emotions play across her face, that whatever reason the other man was no longer in her life must have been a big part of why she'd left her home.

Surprised by the tenderness of his feelings toward her, Lucas wanted nothing more than to reassure this lovely woman that she was safe here. For a brief moment, he wished he could take her in his arms and soothe her, to assure her that she could talk about her past or not. That the only thing he cared about was her comfort.

But he realized that there was every chance it was his own reticence in speaking candidly that may be leading to hers right now.

He had to do something. Say something.

He had to help her somehow, the way she was already helping him.

"What was it like sailing?" he asked gently. "I've never been."

She spun around, eyes shining.

"It was . . ." She looked away again, thinking, trying to find the words for what she wanted to say. "It was utterly magical. Exhilarating and . . . I can't describe it. Being on the ocean is like being in a completely different world. It's an exercise in trust, certainly, without solid earth beneath your feet, but it's worth it. David—my late fiancé—had been before with some of his medical school friends, and he talked about it all the time until we finally got a chance to go together. I'll never forget it."

Lucas did not miss her adding the word "late" to her description of the other man.

"You know," he began, terrified but determined to not let this opportunity slip past him. He didn't know anyone else who carried a pain so similar to his own. "My late wife used to say the same thing about the snow every winter. That it was otherworldly. She grew up in the South and it wasn't until we moved here that she got to experience a true winter. Even after living in Wyoming for six or seven years, she still saw the magic and wonder in it every year. The icicles on the eaves. The light layer of snow highlighting the bare tree branches. Christine was . . . like a little girl in her excitement sometimes."

"I love that," she said softly, turning back and closing the distance between them. "I love the idea of hanging on to a little bit of wonder and not letting the world make us jaded."

Lucas nodded, not trusting himself to speak. He was terribly afraid that becoming jaded was precisely what he'd done in the wake of Christine's death. Despite the example she had left for him of the opposite.

"I think . . . for me, at least," she continued, "all of this ranch life still has the feeling of magic for me. It's so different from what I grew up with—even the gardening."

"Do you think you'll ever get used to it?"

"I'm not sure. There's part of me that hopes I never do, but then I suppose it all depends on how long I'm here."

There were still well over four months left on her contract. Lucas decided that whatever decision was made in September, he would make sure that Miss Sweet had the most magical, exhilarating experience here on the plains that he could offer her.

"Well, in that case," he said, "should we get started? Ready to get your hands dirty again?"

Miss Sweet put the last bite of biscuit in her mouth and nodded, eyes wide with excitement.

"I've been doing this a while and I still get a little bit of a thrill seeing what a mere mortal can do. I've heard it said that farming—or even just a small vegetable garden like this—is God's way of letting man become a creator himself."

"All the food and nourishment we need for the year from those tiny little seeds."

"Exactly. The first thing we need to do though"— Lucas jabbed his shovel into the damp earth at the edge of the garden patch—"is till."

"Why is that?" she asked as she took up her own shovel and stood near him.

"Lots of reasons. For one, it's still pretty damp down beneath the hard top layer of soil," he said as he stabbed the shovel down again. "Turning over a good amount of earth helps dry it out a bit, and mixes up whatever other fertilizer, air, and other nutrients there are to make the ground a better environment for growing."

"I know it's difficult to work and talk," she said, "but would you tell me about what we'll need to do for the animals throughout the summer?"

He smiled, digging up another shovel of dirt as he began.

CHAPTER ELEVEN

The rest of the afternoon passed quickly, far more enjoyable than Jenny ever would have guessed. Somehow during the hours they had spent together, something within Mr. Garrett unlocked. His hard outer shell was softening. Her questions had gotten him talking about what his childhood growing up on a small farm in Tennessee had been like, about what previous years at Prairie Winds Ranch had looked like. She, in turn, answered his questions about living in a city "on top of your neighbors," as he'd described it. The work of tilling the section of land for the vegetable garden had gone by without her hardly noticing.

"But we'll leave the planting for when Mary is feeling better," he'd told her as they reached the final stretch of earth. "It can wait a day, and she seemed so excited. Besides, I know you have plenty of other chores to get to."

"Supper is the only thing that has to be done today,

but you're right. She would be so sad if we did that bit without her."

"It will be a fun project for all three of us."

Jenny felt her heart beat more rapidly under the intensity of his gaze. Thinking about the three of them working together, putting in the seeds for their future meals, made her feel far more excited than chores should. Her face got hot, and she hoped he attributed that to being in the sun and not a blush.

Mr. Garrett cleared his throat and continued. "I've been thinking more about what you said about letting her work alongside me and I think the garden is probably a good opportunity. Something we can work on together."

She nodded, not trusting herself to put words to what she was feeling.

He left her to it, heading back to the barn with the tools while Jenny got to work in the kitchen. She'd done the dishes after breakfast, but still needed to clean the floor. Although she hadn't admitted it, the truth was that being outdoors with the rancher most of the day had set her behind. There was a roast to prepare and vegetables to chop and some kind of dessert to whip up if there was still time. If wondering what Mr. Garrett was up to consumed her thoughts, she did not let it distract from her work.

Teddy and Allan arrived back at the ranch not long before supper, and all three men spent a harried time getting the wagon unloaded before the food was ready. While they unloaded the wagon—Jenny admonishing them to not put too much on Teddy still—she stayed indoors and made room for all the things they had brought home. Loads of flour, rice, beans, sugar, and other dried goods were put away in the pantry. A bolt of green calico to make Mary a new dress and—as Mr. Garrett had promised—the mail.

Jenny had not heard a word from any of her sisters since she'd left Baltimore weeks earlier and was desperately hoping for something. Even though train travel made mail delivery far faster than it had been in generations past, the wait tugged at Jenny's heart. She was used to living side by side with Eliza, Abigail, and Beatrice, seeing them every day, talking to them about all the tiny details of their lives. While she knew that whatever they could fit into a letter would be important, Jenny could not help but mourn whatever smaller stories they would have deemed not important enough to write down.

She missed her sisters. But that was the price she paid to escape her memories.

Though she'd forced herself to be patient, she all but pounced on Mr. Garrett when he entered the kitchen holding two battered envelopes.

"Mail call," he said as she bounded across the room to him.

"From Abigail and Beatrice," she reported, recognizing their handwriting immediately. "I'm not surprised Eliza didn't write. It's impossible to pin that girl down to do anything expected of her."

"I was thinking it's about time we showed you the town. If you have mail you'd like to post to send back to Baltimore, we can go into Juniper Falls again in a few days."

She looked up at him in surprise—only an invitation

like that could have torn her attention away from the letters from her sisters.

"Really? For how long? Will I need to wear something special? Should we eat ahead of time?"

He chuckled. "One question at a time. There's going to be a church picnic on the Saturday before Easter. Some of the businesses will set up booths, like the cafe, and there will be some dancing, some crafts for the children. We can go for the afternoon and stay as long as Mary is awake."

"I would love that. Truly. Thank you so much. I've been so curious about that town since I arrived here."

He held her gaze as he nodded his understanding. "I'm sorry we haven't gone before now."

"It's fine!" She sat at the kitchen table so she could take her time to read the letters. "Really. There's plenty to do on the ranch, and plenty that I still need to learn about. Juniper Falls will always be there and, if I'm honest, I'm glad that I had to wait a bit. I might have been overwhelmed otherwise."

He nodded, holding her gaze for another moment before exiting the kitchen. "All right, then. It's a plan. Enjoy your letters. I'll see you at supper."

While the vegetables and pork slowly roasted, filling the kitchen with their delectable scent, Jenny gave herself the treat of reading her sisters' letters—weather, their father's health, a hint of crossness from a neighbor —instead of making a dessert for the family as she'd originally planned. There was simply too much about her home that she missed. She had just paused and added a tiny bit more fuel to the cast iron stove when Mrs. Potter entered, carrying a fresh apple pie.

"I thought you might like to serve this after supper. My Allan knows how partial I am to the pie from the Sunshine Cafe and brought it back for me, but I'd much rather share."

Jenny could smell the rich, buttery pastry even from where she sat across the room. The scent of sugar and cinnamon laced with apple made her hungry enough to wish they could eat it that moment.

"Oh, goodness! Are you sure? It smells amazing."

"Heavens yes. If I ate this whole thing myself, I'd regret it for a week."

"Thank you," Jenny answered sincerely, rising to take it from her and set it on the counter for later. "So much. That saves me the time of pulling something together myself. I got lost in reading my sisters' letters and now am short on time."

"You must have had a very busy day," Mrs. Potter said, sitting at the kitchen table. "I don't think I saw you more than just that quick dash through the house."

"We repaired stalls in the barn in the morning, and then tilled the garden this afternoon," Jenny said. "Tomorrow, if Mary is feeling better, maybe we'll put all the seeds in. Spring always seemed to sneak up on me when I lived in the city and there's so much more to do here; it's a very different experience here on the plains. So much planning and preparation to be ready when the earth is."

"I admit to being a little sad to see the snow go. Winter was always a big deal here for the Garretts."

"He mentioned that today, actually," Jenny said quietly.

Mrs. Potter looked at her sharply. "Did he?"

Jenny nodded. "He told me that his— that the late Mrs. Garrett loved winter and the snow and that it was a special time for them, when Mary was a baby."

"That it was, my dear. Mind you, I wasn't here full-time when Mrs. Garrett was alive, but we became close over the years. She failed considerably after Mary was born and I came off and on to offer help. As much as they'd let me. I didn't like seeing that little girl suffer because her ma was too tired to make breakfast. Mr. Garrett tried to take care of all of it after she died, but . . . A man can only do so much."

"That's beautiful," Jenny said softly. "What a gift you must have given her in those final years, that assurance that Mary had someone else looking after her."

"I hope so. It was difficult, knowing how badly she wanted to live for her daughter even as her body failed."

"Oh, that poor woman." Jenny let out a long breath, missing her own mother too.

"The hardest part, however, was watching her husband mourn her before she was even gone. It broke my heart. Christine—Mrs. Garrett—knew she didn't have much longer with her family. They all knew. Even Mary seemed to sense it, young though she was. And Mr. Garrett responded by throwing himself even more into work. Always having something else to do than sit by her side, or read to his daughter or . . ."

Mrs. Potter trailed off.

"And then she was gone," Jenny offered.

The older woman nodded grimly. "Mr. Garrett has never said so to me, but it seemed like he was keeping himself away from his dying wife so he didn't have to feel the pain and grief that he knew would find him. And then once she was gone, he regretted all the time he'd missed."

"That sounds like a lot of grieving spouses I've seen. At the hospital. Before that even. It must be so painful to go through that loss every day for weeks or longer. I suppose in some ways I'm lucky that my own fiancé was killed in a sudden accident. Just here one moment and gone the next."

"Oh, you poor dear."

Jenny nodded bravely. "It hurts less and less every day. Being here, being out of Baltimore and meeting you all, has helped more than I expected it to."

"I'm so glad. I suspect a change of scenery might have done Mr. Garrett good as well. Christine confided in me that she was afraid her husband would close off his heart completely when she was gone. She didn't want that for his own sake, but also for Mary's. The girl can't lose both of her parents."

Both women were startled to hear him clear his throat from where he stood at the doorway.

———

"Oh!" Miss Sweet blushed when she saw that he had been close enough to hear their conversation. "Mr. Garrett, we didn't see you there."

Though Lucas felt a tiny bit ashamed that he'd been eavesdropping, this was his house, these were his employees. He had every right to know what they might be saying about him or his family. He stood up a little straighter.

"And on that note," Mrs. Potter said briskly,

pretending any discomfort or tension was nonexistent, "I think I will go check on the girl in question. You know Teddy won't bat an eye if she eats all of the candy he brought her before supper."

The older woman swept out the door toward the living room, leaving Lucas alone with Jenny.

"Mr. Garrett," she said quietly. "I'm so sorry. We shouldn't have— Your past is your own and—"

He shook his head, forestalling her apologies. "I'm not angry. How can I be when Mrs. Potter is exactly right? I . . . I made mistakes. And Christine knew me well enough to be able to guess what mistakes I might make in the future too. In hindsight, that might be part of why I stayed away. She was always wanting to talk to me about a future that she was not in, what I should be doing for Mary, for myself, and I . . . I couldn't bear it. I didn't want to face it."

"It seems like she really loved you."

"She did. Far more than I deserve."

"The ones who love us see us more clearly, don't they?" she said softly. "David died . . . suddenly. Unexpectedly. He didn't have a chance to tell me what he hoped for me after he was gone, but there was a time, the last Christmas we had together, when he got a blank journal to write in. Apparently I had talked in the past about wanting to write a book. I didn't even remember telling him that, but he paid attention."

Lucas smiled. "That's really thoughtful."

"I didn't think I had that kind of project in me, but he did. He believed in me and wanted to support my efforts. He offered me a future with that gift. That knowing, that . . . being seen by another person is hard to get used to."

"That might be why I've been . . . hesitant about some things," he said. "I apologize if you've felt neglected or abandoned. I want you to feel at home here, but . . ."

"I know," she said softly. "Please don't feel the need to explain or apologize. We both have our reasons."

"I enjoyed today, though," he said, taking another step toward her. "I never would have thought it, but it was . . . today was nice. Thank you for sharing your day with me."

"Thank you."

He hesitated to say more; he'd already burdened her so much with his past and pain and problems. Now was not the time to let himself get sentimental. Shaking himself out of his memories, Lucas changed the subject.

"I actually came back in here because the boys brought a treat back for you as well." He held out a small gift box, a lovely dark brown with a cheerful red ribbon tied around it in a bow. "Penny candy for Mary. The apple pie for Mrs. Potter. And, if I recognize this packaging, it looks like they brought you caramels from Sugar and Spice Bakery."

"Oh!" she exclaimed, crossing the kitchen floor in two long steps in her excitement. "Oh, how delightful. I'll have to thank them, what a surprise. Everyone has just been so kind to me since I got here, Mr. Garrett. I appreciate all of you so much. It means the world to me after— After Baltimore."

Lucas could not help but soften toward her after hearing about the tragedy that had driven her from her home and family. No wonder she'd been so excited to see the town and perhaps meet new people who could help her plant a new life in the West. He wanted to help her feel more at home.

"Call me Lucas."

Her eyes did not leave his as she took a deep breath. "Jenny."

He nodded.

"Would you like a caramel?" she asked in an exaggerated whisper. "Quickly before anybody else walks in?"

He laughed at her pretended subterfuge. It had been a very long time since Lucas had found the fun in small things like this. It had been a gift of Christine's, and now seeing the same trait in Miss Sweet—Jenny—he felt more at home with himself than he had in years.

CHAPTER TWELVE

The treats that Allan and Teddy had brought back from Juniper Falls were the perfect cap to a satisfying day, a light celebration that reminded her how special this place was. Even Mary's brief illness couldn't mar Jenny's thoughts about how well this experiment was going for her. She'd left her home with only the vaguest of expectations about what her new life would look like, and now she found herself truly learning to care about every person who lived at Prairie Winds Ranch. She had found herself a family.

She was putting in good, honest work, and her reward was a freedom from the heaviness of her past. If sometimes she wondered how David's family and others who loved him were faring, she never let herself linger on those thoughts very long. The past had to stay in the past.

It was time for new beginnings. Time to look forward into this new life she was building.

And that included getting better at gardening.

By breakfast the next day, Mary was feeling much better. She came to the breakfast table early with everyone else, sat next to her father, and looked hungrily at the plate of bacon that Jenny placed on the table. As Teddy and Allan planned out their tasks for the day, Jenny served Mary's breakfast and told her about their own plans.

"You sure your doll isn't sniffly anymore?"

Mary shook her head. "She's feeling much better."

"In that case . . . Do you want to help me and your papa with something today?"

Mary nodded, her mouth full of eggs.

"We waited until you were feeling better, but today is the day we plant the garden. The earth is all ready for us. We just need to put in the seeds."

Mary swallowed quickly. "Really? Papa too?"

She looked excitedly at her father, who chuckled at her enthusiasm. "Is that all right with you, pet? I know it's something you and Miss Sweet were working on together, but if you'll let me—"

"Yes, please!"

Jenny met Lucas's eyes across the table. She grinned; Mary was even more enthusiastic than she'd expected.

To be honest, Lucas's interest in gardening with them was also far more than she'd expected. Something was changing in him, she thought. And she was grateful for that.

Though she could not say what it meant for her position here, for the six months she was contracted or even for her relationship with Mary, over the past couple of days it had become clear that Lucas Garrett was beginning to thaw. Where he had been distant when she'd first arrived, now he was teasing and laughing with his daughter, making an effort to spend time with her. And Jenny. Her first impression of him had been so very different.

Over the previous weeks, Jenny had done her best to hold herself back, to not pressure him in any way or have expectations of closeness. She was an employee there to fulfill the requirements of her position. And yet, even with their mutual hesitation and wariness, their intimacy had progressed.

She found herself strangely nervous about spending another day working alongside him. There was still so much he didn't know about her, and she him.

"After breakfast," Jenny said as she sat to eat, "we'll find our gloves and fill the canteens, and the three of us will spend the day out in the vegetable patch."

Mary turned serious, turning her entire body in her chair to face her father. "Papa, I think we should plant strawberries."

"You do, do you? That wouldn't be because you like to put them on your pancakes, would it?"

"Teddy likes them on his pancakes."

Teddy chuckled at this.

"That's true, he does." Lucas grinned at his ranch hand.

"And we like Teddy. We want him to like it here."

Lucas laughed. "We do, yes."

"What else do you think we should plant?" Jenny asked her.

"Umm . . ." Mary looked around, and then up at her. "I dunno. Carrots? Flibbit likes carrots."

"We have seeds for carrots. And onions and potatoes

and corn. Green beans. Pumpkins. What's your favorite vegetable?"

She shrugged.

"Well," Jenny said with a laugh, "we'll have to try a bunch of them so you can decide."

"But what if I only like strawberries?"

"We'll figure out what to do if that happens," she assured the little girl. "No sense in borrowing trouble, right? We never know what the future can bring."

"All right," Mary said a little doubtfully. "As long as there's strawberries."

Accordingly, once breakfast was finished and the dishes washed and put away—Mary helped dry—the three of them headed out to the garden. The day before, Jenny and Lucas had cleared and tilled a patch of land that was large enough to support food for not just the six of them, but a little bit more. Lucas had advised enlarging the area when they were tilling, noting that the extra space would be only a little more work and would provide a safe buffer in case of drought, disease, or animal thieves.

"You know how to can, I assume? For when we end up with far more corn than anyone can eat?" he'd asked her.

To which Jenny replied that it was a good thing Mrs. Potter was still around to teach her. She'd learned plenty of skills in her work as a nurse, but that meant there were blind-spots in her homemaking.

"I'll ask her," Jenny had assured him. "I don't mind looking a bit foolish when needed."

There was much to do at every step of the process. And now, as they went row by row putting in the seeds for a variety of edible plants, she reached out to dig out another tiny hole in the earth in which to drop a seed and pushed herself a little too far. She had been squatting in the dirt, her skirts piled up around her, reaching with a trowel in one hand and a collection of carrot seeds held carefully in the other. Reaching, reaching, reaching . . .

But her balance couldn't accommodate such stretching out.

Not wanting to drop all the seeds in an effort to spare herself a soft landing, Jenny lost her balance. She tried windmilling her arms to regain it but fell—excruciatingly slowly—on her right side into the dirt. She smashed the careful trench Mary had been digging.

"Oh no!" the little girl cried.

"Are you all right?" Lucas asked, hurrying to help her up.

Jenny felt only a little bit embarrassed; she could see the humor in her absurdity.

"Ah well," she said with a laugh. "I did tell you I don't mind looking a bit foolish. Let's try that again."

"Leave the seeds," Lucas told her as he helped her up. "One thing at a time, maybe."

It was possibly the first time she had noticed their hands touch. His were dirty, rough, but warm. Strong. Immediately Jenny felt as though she could trust this man to take care of them if the situation called for it. She caught something in his expression that made her blush, but he quickly turned away again, back to where he had been working.

Lucas had been working at the far end of the vegetable patch, digging a narrow trench for seeds parallel to the edge of the turned earth. He had been calculating how long this project would take, and if he would have time to check on the herd before it got dark.

When Jenny gasped in surprise, he looked up. As he watched, she laughed at herself, sprawled in the dirt after losing her balance. He hurried to her side to check if she was hurt and to help her up.

"One thing at a time, maybe," he said, pulling her to her feet.

Her small, soft hands in his made him feel . . . something. Something that he was not prepared for, that he had not felt in years. This was a joyful, sweet woman who he found himself wanting to spend more time with. Wanting to take care of and make happy in some way.

This was *not* why he had hired a housekeeper, though.

Once she was steady on her feet again, he turned away, back to his own tasks and away from that beautiful smile that was so magnetizing it drove all other thoughts from his mind.

Back on her feet, Jenny brushed all the dirt off herself and helped Mary fix the holes she had been digging. Mary made a tentative joke, teasing Jenny, and lit up with pleasure when the latter laughed.

This whole afternoon was shaping up to be even more pleasant than he'd expected. A couple of months earlier, during the darkest part of winter, Lucas had had an attack of second thoughts, wondering if bringing a stranger into his daughter's life was really the best solution to his problems. But now that he saw them interacting, saw how much Mary was blossoming under Jenny's attention, he could let himself enjoy it too.

When was the last time he had laughed so much while doing chores around the ranch? When was the last time he had let himself be honest about having any kind of feelings other than worry about the ranch, Mary, and their future?

There was a magic to Jenny Sweet. She was helping the Garretts find joy in life again.

He found himself thinking ahead to the fall season with her here. To Christmas. To Mary's next birthday and all number of changes ahead—well past the end of her current contract.

How had they ever gotten by without her?

He caught Jenny's eye and realized he had been staring.

"Why are you looking at me like that?" she said, dusting the last loose bits of dirt off her skirt and. She crossed to where he was, some ten or fifteen yards away from Mary, glancing over her shoulder to check on the girl every few steps.

There was a soft smile on her face, a twinkle in her eye as though there was some secret they shared. He could not help but warm under her joyful approach to life, finding himself wanting to feel her touch again.

Even so, he couldn't tell her any of these things. He wasn't even sure he wanted to warm up to anyone at all.

He cleared his throat and got back to work digging a trench for seeds.

"Looking at you like what?"

"Like I am a circus clown who just got a pie in the face."

He laughed despite himself. "It was rather silly. You didn't even put your hands out to help yourself."

"The seeds!" she exclaimed defensively.

"I know. Like not ducking when a pie is coming at your face."

Jenny sputtered, knowing she was being teased, and ended up simply laughing along with him.

"All right then. Next time I make a pie, we'll see what you do about it."

Her grin, with the afternoon sun behind her, the warm spring air and scent of wildflowers all around, made him catch his breath. The promise of any kind of fun with her gave him something to look forward to.

When he didn't respond with words, she squatted down in the dirt next to him, beginning to dig more spots for seeds with the trowel she still held. They worked side by side in silence for a few minutes before she spoke again.

"Thank you for helping with this today," she said. "And yesterday. I know that there's so much to do around here that could have kept you busy."

"Of course. It's not as though it is wasted time and . . . forgive me for saying, but it was a pleasure to learn about you more. Since we're sleeping under the same roof and all."

They both paused in their work; he had a hard time dragging his gaze away to focus on what he was supposed to be doing. All he could think about was spending more time with this woman.

"And thank you for telling me about your wife," she added, quietly enough that Mary would not be able to hear. "I know firsthand what it's like to lose someone who you thought would be in your life forever."

"Thank you for understanding that it's not easy to talk about. Is that . . ." He looked down. "Is . . . is that why you left Baltimore?"

"Yes. There was just too much of my life tied up with memories of him and I was no good to anyone. I truly admire your ability to remain here where— I can't imagine how difficult the last few years have been."

"Thank you. They have, but," he looked at his daughter who was digging happily, "just having Mary helps."

He paused, wondering if he should say more.

But in the smile she offered him he saw the truth— he didn't have to say more. Jenny understood him completely. She understood the pain that he had been through, and now the future that he looked forward to.

Having such a woman—a friend—by his side was going to be an immense improvement from the previous few years, he had no doubt.

CHAPTER THIRTEEN

"Miss Sweet, are you excited to go into town today?" Mary asked as Jenny put the platter of pancakes in the middle of the breakfast table. "Papa said I can pick out a new toy at the general store. Do you know what a paper doll is? I think I might pick out a paper doll!"

"I am very excited to go into town." She brought over the pot of coffee, topping off the mugs of all three men before finally taking her seat. It was such a delight to see Mary so excited, coming out of her shell. Jenny was looking forward to the day together. "And I love paper dolls. I'd be happy to play with them with you if you'd like."

"Oh, yes!"

"Do you know I have never been to Juniper Falls?"

Mary's eyes got wide. "Never?"

Jenny shook her head. "Never. And I bet you have been a bunch of times. What's your favorite part?"

"I think this can be a conversation for the drive into

town," Lucas suggested. "You and Miss Sweet still need to get dressed before we leave. Finish your breakfast, pet."

Mary rushed to get ready in her excitement, the family piled into one wagon, and they were soon on their way into Juniper Falls. The Prairie Winds Ranch sat a few miles outside of the town and, as they drew closer, Jenny noticed at least half a dozen other wagons full of families traveling in from the surrounding countryside. The church picnic that day must be a bigger draw than Lucas had implied; she was thrilled for the chance to experience every drop of it.

As they approached the center of town, Jenny felt like her head was on a swivel, looking in every direction, trying to catch snatches of conversation from those she passed by, making reminders to herself to come back soon so she could visit the seamstress or the cafe or the hardware store, even. She had letters tucked into the pocket of her coat that she would leave with the post-master at the general store, and she anticipated a full day of activity and new friends.

There were one primary, wide street that ran east to west through the center of Juniper Falls, with two more crossing perpendicularly and more narrow streets expanding out and creating the broader grid. It wasn't until she was here—surrounded by the people and the action—that she realized there was a bit of Baltimore she did miss. Living on a ranch in a rural setting was a delightful change to what she was used to, but returning to even a small town like this energized her. She wanted to see everything and do everything she could in the few hours they would be visiting. Church and maybe volunteering at the school and browsing the general store and so much else.

She would be sure to come back into Juniper Falls often, if she could. Maybe when Mary started going to school, she could make it a regular excursion. Once she had a better grasp of the rhythm of the seasons and her duties at the ranch, she could plan for a trip into town.

As soon as possible.

As Lucas drove the wagon through the town to the farther side, he told Jenny a bit about the place.

"Well, you know we're here for Easter, but really Juniper Falls has all kinds of gatherings all year. The hotel is surprisingly busy for a town without a rail station."

"What kind of gatherings?" she asked as she watched two young boys walking down the boardwalk with their dog.

"Soon, in the summer, we have the Golden Days Festival and close down these streets entirely to allow for space for dancing and games and things. It's a chance to celebrate the growing season and take advantage of the longest days of sunlight. A lot of the shopkeepers donate refreshments and decorations, and folks come from miles around to celebrate the long days and growing harvest. It's one of the biggest events we have. You'll love it. I heard that Mr. Brown will be selling the inn, though, so it will be interesting to see what happens with that."

"I would love a festival like that." Her eyes lit up. She noticed the intricate weather vane on top of the inn when they drove past. "Even though we had our church and our neighborhood in Baltimore, it's still a big city. A lot more strangers. This is so much more . . . homey."

"That's good." He grinned at her as he guided the team down a different street toward the church. "I hope you feel at home here."

There were more private homes in this part of the town, more gardens. The church was situated a couple of blocks from the main street, with the parsonage tucked away behind it and a vast spread of grass in between. Though it was still relatively early in the day, when they arrived at the church and the grassy park beyond, there were already several families setting up their blankets, picnic baskets, and even games.

"Oh!" Jenny said, seeing the activity. "Were we supposed to bring a picnic lunch? You didn't tell me. I didn't pack anything for us at all."

"Not to worry," Lucas assured her.

He drew the wagon to a stop near where other men had tied their horses, hitching rails all along the road. There was a tall, lanky young man helping to take care of the teams while wagons were unloaded and families spread out. Jenny climbed down from the wagon and crossed to where Lucas was helping his daughter down. Teddy moved to help with the horses, and Allan strode off down the road toward the center of town.

"I thought you might appreciate a day off, actually," he continued. "Allan is going to the Sunshine Cafe to get us food now. A few of the families do that, and Mrs. Jenkins is well equipped to feed extras. This way you don't have to think about it at all and can just enjoy your day. There's plenty here to occupy you without also adding on feeding this bunch."

"That's really thoughtful. Thank you so much."

He nodded, seeming a little embarrassed at the praise. "I'm trying to get better at . . . enjoying life. Instead of working all the time. Someone told me that it would be good for my daughter to see, at least. So, we'll take a day off together."

Jenny blushed, flattered that he remembered her words this many weeks later. Before she could respond, however, Mary called out loudly.

"Papa, there's Nellie Griffin!" she exclaimed. "Can I go play with her?"

Teddy had already taken over managing the team for Lucas, and the latter offered Jenny his arm to lead her toward where the picnic was taking shape and the families were settling in.

"You ready to meet some of our neighbors?"

Jenny felt suddenly frightened, as though this would be an irreversible step that anchored her in this new life. As long as only the residents of Prairie Winds Ranch knew her, she could always return to Baltimore with few repercussions. But making friends, becoming a known neighbor of Juniper Falls, meant that she was betting on herself, betting that this would be her home for longer than the short six-month contract. Despite everything she had told herself about not wanting to return to the East, the fact was that Baltimore, Maryland, and the community of her childhood felt familiar and safe, and in the back of her mind it always felt like an option. Not her first choice, but an option nevertheless.

Today's adventure at the church picnic in Juniper Falls would change all of that.

"I'm ready," she said, with more conviction than she felt.

"Come this way. The first person I think you'll love is Edith Bennett. She runs a boarding house and has been here about a decade, I think. Makes amazing sugar cookies."

Jenny squared her shoulders and followed him to a little knot of kind-looking folks talking around a table set with a big serving bowl of lemonade and mismatched cups.

———

Lucas felt unexpectedly proud to be arriving at the Easter weekend church picnic with Miss Jenny Sweet on his arm. He was lucky to know her at all, and now he was doubly lucky for the privilege of introducing her to the rest of his community.

He knew her to be compassionate and charming, and so was perfectly confident in her ability to make new friends. And in doing so, Lucas realized he hoped her amiableness would reflect well on him, on his ability to find a caregiver for his daughter and his own character judgment in offering her the position. For the last several years—since Christine had died—Lucas had held himself apart from the families that knew and cared about him, unwilling to be seen grieving, vulnerable. Now, with Jenny in Wyoming, he felt himself warming to the idea of being social again.

While this was ostensibly a church picnic, anyone

was welcome, including families like the Garretts who only came into town for a worship service every few months. Pastor Langdon was one of the kindest, most understanding and welcoming men Lucas had ever met, and his wife went above and beyond to be a model wife and mother for the community. As a pair—along with their two children—they made anyone looking for a bit of family fun and camaraderie want to spend the day here.

After a while, Allan returned from the Sunshine Cafe with cheese sandwiches, pickled hard-boiled eggs, and cookies for the whole Prairie Winds Ranch group. His family. Mrs. Potter had remembered to bring two of her most worn quilts and set them out on the grass for seating, where they ate out of the cardboard boxes Mrs. Jenkins had packed the food in. The sunshine and cool breeze of the day, coming off the surrounding plains, was the perfect environment to pique his appetite.

Over their late afternoon meal, Mary would not stop talking to Jenny. Telling her all about her friend Nellie, about the games they played, about how Nellie was getting new paper on the walls in her room. He watched with pleasure as Jenny asked her questions and took the child's every enthusiasm as seriously as she might that of an adult. It was almost surprising to learn that Jenny had not raised any other children before now; she was so naturally gifted in this kind of nurturing and support.

But Jenny did more than simply watch and listen in the face of all these new people. He really should have expected as much, after the way that she had stepped up to care for Teddy's wound, to help himself with the barn repairs. When she saw a need—any need, even that of a stranger—Jenny did everything she could to meet it.

The first thing Lucas noticed was her sharing her cookies from the cafe with old Mr. Sharp. He had been widowed earlier in the winter and came walking up to the picnic on his own, with just his cane in his hands. His son ran the *Juniper Falls Gazette*, and so must have been too busy that day to accompany him. Lucas did not overhear the conversation, he just saw Jenny approach him slowly, kindly, asking after him. The next thing he knew, she had run back to where they'd been sitting on the quilt, grabbed her small cardboard box with the rest of her lunch, and ran back to Mr. Sharp. He could tell from her gesturing that she was offering him to sit with them as well, but he refused.

When she came back to their seats on her own, Lucas asked her what he had said that had driven her to such action.

"He was telling me about his late wife, how last year at this picnic she had brought enough cookies for all the children. How much he missed her. I imagine his son and daughter-in-law might have done the same for him if they had heard him talk about it the way I did."

"That's really kind."

She shrugged, smiling under the praise. "It's what anyone would do, I suspect."

Later, when Daisy Lambert stumbled during the three-legged race, Jenny was the first to help her to her feet and bandage her twisted ankle. When the blacksmith, Tom Coulter, had lamented about the injuries that kept occurring in his shop, Jenny offered to go to the general store with him and teach him what salves and bandages he could use if the worst happened.

She had compliments for Mrs. Jenkins's cooking and for Mrs. Langdon's lemonade. She made tentative plans with Mrs. Frye to come volunteer at the school and promised the man from the livery that she wanted to learn how to ride.

As the afternoon drew closer to sunset, a space in the grass was cleared for dancing. The musicians were warming up their instruments and Lucas felt a peace that had eluded him for years. Even before Christine had died, he had spent years worried about her. Now, though, with all of that behind him, he could look forward to the future with a confidence he had forgotten.

And he wanted to share that with Jenny. She was the reason he could let loose and feel optimistic for the first time in so long.

He got to his feet, and she followed, brushing the few little pieces of grass off her skirt.

"Where to now?" she asked, looking around with interest.

"Will you dance with me?"

He took her hand and gently tugged her toward the open space where couples were beginning to gather. The musicians had started playing a basic waltz, and Lucas was strangely excited for this chance. His toes seemed to be tapping to the music on their own.

"A dance?" She looked around wildly.

"Just one or two," he said. "Stretch our legs a bit? I'm probably not as fine a dance partner as you might have had in Baltimore, but—"

"I—I can't." She pulled her hand away, shaking her

head before offering Lucas what he knew was a false smile. "I'm ever so sorry, but I told Mr. Coulter I would teach him a little bit about treating burns and things. I'm to meet him at the general store now, actually, before we go back. I'm so sorry."

He watched her go without protesting, disappointed. There was more than just her promise to Mr. Coulter, but Lucas was too dismayed to let himself think about it.

CHAPTER FOURTEEN

They all got back to the ranch late that night, Lucas insisting on putting his daughter to bed so Jenny could truly enjoy a full day off from her duties. While she was grateful for that kindness, she lay awake for a bit after she'd gone to bed, thinking about her reaction to Lucas asking her to dance while at the picnic. She hoped she'd not come off too rude, but the truth was that meeting all those people was a big step for her, and she could not be ready for another big step that same day. She thought over their interaction from several angles, hoping she had not hurt his feelings, while also recognizing the uncertainty that still remained.

But she wasn't kept awake long; the day had thoroughly exhausted her even without having to cook and look after Mary as closely. Going into Juniper Falls, meeting so many of the men and women who adored Lucas, and feeling like she was making her own mark on the community gave her a sense of satisfaction that she had not felt in . . . months. A year, perhaps? Before David had died, certainly. She sank into her mattress and finally drifted off to sleep, grateful for the life she now had to look forward to.

Grateful, too, that she was finally able to fall asleep. Jenny had to wake early enough the next morning to make breakfast for everyone at the ranch before they drove into town again for the Easter Sunday worship service.

"Going into town two days in a row?" Jenny said, teasing Lucas as she filled his coffee cup. Despite her worry, there did not seem to be any tension between them. "Such luxury. Such extravagance. How ever will I settle down to normal life after this?"

The ranch hands had finished their breakfast, cleared their plates, and were heading to their bunkhouse to put on their Sunday best. Mary and Mrs. Potter were still finishing their own breakfasts when Jenny got the chance to finally sit down and eat.

"If it's too much for you, I am happy to let you stay behind," Lucas said, clearing his own plate. "I know you've gotten used to only seeing a couple faces every day."

"Don't you dare leave me behind, Lucas Garrett." Jenny buttered her biscuit, intending to eat quickly so she could finish getting ready. "I don't know how you can stand not attending church every Sunday, but I'm so grateful that we're going for Easter. It was so nice meeting everyone yesterday."

"I'll try to take you more often this summer," he promised, and Jenny felt a thrill go all through her. "It takes up the whole day, but if you'd like to make an effort, we can."

This intention for the future, this looking ahead, was just one more way that she was putting down roots here in Wyoming. It scared her, but she had done far harder things in the past.

The family was in the wagon and heading down the road not much later that morning, and Jenny relived her experience of the previous day's trip into town. Of course, there were far fewer folks on the streets of Juniper Falls on a Sunday morning than a Saturday afternoon, but she still sensed the same community and palpable joy that she'd experienced the day before.

It was all exactly as she could wish. Even before reaching the church building, Jenny sent up a silent little prayer of gratitude that this could be her life. This could be her future. She just had to be brave enough for what that meant.

For the service that morning, Pastor Langdon preached on the hope inherent in Easter, the new beginning promised by Christ rising from the dead. As she sat in the pew between Mrs. Potter and Lucas, alongside her neighbors and new friends, Jenny felt the peace of her own new beginning. David Watts would always be part of her life, part of her past and her years in medicine, but Juniper Falls was her future.

She was sure of it, and the tentative dreams and desires were beginning to solidify. When Lucas had asked her to dance the night before she'd been scared, not wanting to get too attached, but after sitting through Pastor Langdon's message, Jenny felt herself leaning into the uncertainty of that promised future.

There was still a lot about this new life in Juniper Falls for her to learn about. And a lot for her to look forward to.

After the benediction, when the congregation began to break up and file out of the church building, Jenny stuck close to Lucas's side. She had met a good number of these folks, and she was generally skilled at remembering names, but it was still a lot all at once. He guided her to a circle of couples and introduced her all around. These were the parents of Mary's friends, and families that Jenny should get to know.

As she stood and chatted, learning their children's names and where each family lived, she heard her name from elsewhere. It distracted her, surprising her simply because she wasn't certain many people in Juniper Falls knew her yet. Of the dozens of folks she'd met the day before, how many of them could have committed her name to memory, let alone be talking about her to someone else?

But when she looked to see who was talking about her, she froze in terror, completely deaf to the conversation she was part of.

Jenny's stomach dropped. What was he doing here?

Near to the road, where two different couples seemed poised to walk home after the service, a tall, familiar man with an unkempt blond beard was gesticulating angrily. Whatever peace and serenity the rest of the congregation had gained from the Easter worship service had missed this man entirely. He clearly had something important he needed to say.

But Jenny was not surprised by that. As long as she had known him—several years at this point—Ethan

Watts had been extreme in his emotions. When he had fallen in love it was hard and fast, proposing after only a week. When he had been turned down by that poor harassed girl, he had become despondent and destructive.

As Ethan was David's younger brother, she had been sympathetic to his plights, even while she could not help but see all the ways he was making his own life more difficult.

And now somehow, impossibly, that distraught, passionate young man was here.

Talking about her to people she did not know.

What was Ethan doing in the Wyoming Territory at all, let alone Juniper Falls? The fact that she heard him say her name meant that this was no coincidence.

Jenny suspected the worst.

She couldn't hear more than a few snatches of conversation from this distance, but it was not difficult to guess the gist of what was being said. A big part of why she'd left Baltimore was because of the way Ethan had come after her, bullying and blaming after his brother David had been killed.

Did Ethan Watts really despise her so much as to travel all the way to the Wyoming Territory to destroy her reputation?

"I said we'll have Mary over to spend the night some-time," Mrs. Dixon said, cutting into Jenny's thoughts.

"Oh!" She turned back to the conversation she'd ostensibly been part of. "I'm so sorry. I thought I heard my name and was miles away. What were you asking?"

But she only barely heard these women asking about Mary's plans over the summer, before she enrolled in school. Her attention was still with Ethan, with what he might be saying about her, with what this could mean for her future in Juniper Falls.

What it could mean about her connection to Lucas.

"I'm so sorry. Mr. Garrett and I will have to talk about it and see. I'm sure Mary would love any one of these plans though. I'm so sorry. I think I need— Excuse me."

She left the circle and walked closer to where Ethan was still talking and gesticulating. She had not yet crept close enough to hear what he was saying when Lucas caught up with her.

———

"Jenny?" He touched her elbow gently to get her attention. It was clear her mind was elsewhere. "What is it? Is there anything wrong?"

Jenny looked behind her again toward the knot of people she'd been talking to. "No. No. Nothing. Let's just go. Please. I'm tired and there's still so much to do for supper tonight. Let's go home. Away from here."

Lucas noticed that several of the people in that small group were watching them, their expressions a mix of hostility and curiosity.

"You're sure?"

"Please."

He nodded, offered her his arm, and led her toward the wagon. "We'll get you situated so you can rest, and then I'll go find the others. We'll go right home."

"Thank you."

It pained him to hear the fear in her voice but without more of an invitation he hesitated to question her. He thought they'd made some kind of progress toward true honesty with each other, but maybe he'd been mistaken.

Or maybe, he realized once he had helped her into the wagon and left her on her own, maybe whatever was wrong was too much for her to handle right now. Maybe she just needed time and grace. The good Lord knew that Lucas himself had been given such understanding for years since his wife had died. Maybe Jenny needed a similar gift.

He found Allan and Teddy with Jack Kinsey, of the livery, inspecting some aspect of the bit that Flibbit had in her mouth.

"You boys about ready to go? Miss Sweet wants to get home to start supper."

"Is that the Miss Sweet that let a man die right in front of her?" Jack asked.

"Criminy!" Teddy exclaimed, looking at his friend in shock.

"Excuse me?" Lucas asked, taken aback.

"Yeah, that's what that man said. Not saying I believe it, but . . . He seemed pretty sure."

He pointed toward the road where there was a cluster of people talking urgently, one gesticulating more wildly than the others. In the few moments that Lucas watched, he attracted another couple of listeners to his circle.

"How did you respond?" he asked Jack.

He shrugged. "Didn't rightly know what to say. I don't know the woman, and you yourself admit you only corresponded with her briefly before bringing her out here, didn't you?"

"Are you questioning my judgment?" Lucas felt his temper rising.

"No. No, sir, just admitting that I don't know all the information. I don't know if I even talked to Miss Sweet yesterday. I'm just repeating what I heard."

"And what does that man know about it? I've never seen him before."

"Says he knew her back East. He said the city, but I forget."

"Baltimore."

"That's right. Baltimore. Says he's known her a long time. Knows her family. Sounded like he knew far more than me about her, at least."

Lucas seethed, wanting to throttle whoever that man was disparaging Jenny, but also wanting to confront Jenny about who would possibly come all the way to an Easter Sunday service in Wyoming to do so.

There was something here that he wasn't privy to. While he would have to consider how he'd broach the subject with Jenny, he didn't want Jack to think any more about it.

"You boys ready?" he asked his ranch hands again. "Miss Sweet is in the wagon. I'll go get Mary and meet you there."

He strode away without waiting for an agreement from any of the men. It wasn't Jack's fault. As he said, he was just repeating what he'd heard. The problem came from whatever had possessed this blond man to come after her at all.

Either this stranger had a legitimate grievance

against Jenny and she'd kept whatever it was from him, or this stranger was raving mad and had fixated on her for some reason.

Without knowing more about it, Lucas was at a loss what to do. He could not believe what the stranger was saying. Not of Jenny.

CHAPTER FIFTEEN

While Mary chatted happily with Teddy and Mrs. Potter on the drive back to Prairie Winds Ranch, Jenny remained silent, thoughtful, considering what she had seen in the church yard that morning. Up front, driving the wagon, Lucas seemed to be doing some thinking as well, but she was far too occupied with her own worries to notice anything else.

She had so badly wanted to put all of it behind her—Baltimore, David, her failure—but now Ethan had shown up practically on her new doorstep and insisted she face the disaster of her past. The rest of the afternoon, while coaxing Mary to lay down for a rest, while peeling the potatoes for supper, while bringing Mrs. Potter tea, Jenny turned the problem over and over in her mind.

She didn't think she could keep this secret from Lucas.

Nor did she want to. It was too big, too significant.

Just as David's life and love was part of her past—the

broad strokes of which she'd shared with Lucas—so, too, was his death. She could not escape her guilt over her own part in it. There was no path forward with Lucas, with this family, if she was keeping secrets that so profoundly affected her choices.

She would find a quiet moment and admit everything to him. Scary though that prospect was, Jenny had to trust that he would understand. She would make him understand.

After supper, Mrs. Potter and Mary settled in on the settee in front of the big living room fireplace to read more from *Little Women* while the boys retired to their bunkhouse for the night. Jenny was left alone with Lucas in the kitchen only a short moment, as she started washing the dishes. He had brought over his empty teacup and was just about to exit when she seized her chance to finally unburden herself of the secret that had been consuming her all day.

"Lucas," she ventured before he, too, left her alone to the kitchen.

"Hm?" He paused in the doorway. Jenny gathered all her courage to say what she needed to say.

"Do you have a minute? Can I tell you something, just the two of us?"

"Of course."

She sighed, letting the platter that she'd been scrubbing sink to the bottom of her wash tub. "It's about . . . Well, a lot of things. Baltimore, and what happened at church this morning and . . . I'm just afraid—"

Her voice cracked and she was having a difficult time keeping the tears from flowing. Jenny turned from her task, grabbing a towel to dry her hands. The distraction gave her a moment to collect her thoughts and choose her words carefully. She bowed her head, sensing Lucas watching her closely, though he stayed quiet, respectful, waiting for her to continue in her own time. That gentleness—hidden though it was under his rough exterior—was one of her most cherished discoveries of this position in Wyoming. She would miss it, and him, very much if she was forced to leave. But neither could she continue with this secret between them.

"I just—" she continued. "I know that this is a temporary contract, and you can dissolve the position for any reason, but I didn't want you to think— That is, I don't want to keep secrets from you, and I don't want you to maybe hear rumors or stories from anyone else before you hear it from me."

"All right."

She peered up at him but couldn't read his expression. Had he already heard what Ethan had been saying about her around town?

She took a deep breath.

"Why don't we sit down?" he offered gently.

"Please. Yes. Thank you."

The dining room table in the next room still held some of the platters and serving bowls, but the smaller kitchen table was clear, a low flame flickering in the oil lamp in the center of the table. Jenny slipped into her usual seat, Lucas into his at the head of the table. They were only a few inches apart and though Jenny wanted so badly to reach out to him, to have him hold her hand, comforting and supportive, she held herself back. She would wait to see how he took the news.

With her hands clasped tightly in her lap, Jenny cleared her throat and continued.

"I told you my fiancé David died suddenly. What I didn't tell you was how . . ."

"Oh, Jenny . . ."

"Don't. Please. Don't say anything yet. Just . . . let me get this all out. It's going to be hard enough as it is. Please."

In response, Lucas reached out his hand, offering it to her. Exactly what she had been silently wishing for. There was part of Jenny that felt like she shouldn't. Like she didn't deserve any kind of support or understanding from this good man. But there was a bigger part of her that needed that anchor, that needed the grounding here in Wyoming, in the present moment.

"Thank you," she whispered, and slipped her smaller hand into his large one.

He wrapped his fingers around hers, gently giving her a tiny squeeze, and nodded for her to continue.

"He, um . . . David was a doctor. We met while we were both working at the hospital— I might have mentioned that to you. We lived in the same neighborhood and could walk to work together. It was . . . truly it was one of my favorite little routines in my life. A few minutes of quiet and connection before the bustle of a busy hospital. There's a lot of reasons I have been so affected by his death . . . One of them is the fact that those precious memories of our mornings together are now marred by the memory of that last morning.

"So, well . . . We were walking, hand in hand, down one of the busier streets in Baltimore and suddenly I was pushed to the side, and he was torn from me, and—"

The tears flowed freely now. None of this was easy to say, but now that she'd started, she could not stop.

"He was hit and then dragged by a runaway carriage. He had so many injuries. When I finally caught up to him, I didn't even know where to start. There was a huge gash in his side . . . I was reminded of it when Teddy got rammed by that fence rail a few weeks ago. The broken rib. The bleeding. David's tragedy all came back to me at that moment. It's a wonder I was able to think clearly enough to help Teddy at all."

She smiled sadly.

"But I'm so glad I was able to do for Teddy what I could not for David." A sob escaped her, but she forced herself to continue. "There was so many more injuries than just a broken rib. When I finally pushed through the crowd to him, he was already unconscious and bleeding, and there were broken limbs and so much blood. The people let me through, to his side, but . . . I . . . I don't know. I tried, I know I tried, but it's all a blur now in my memory. I couldn't stop the bleeding quickly enough and he slipped away right in front of me, before I could even . . ."

She let the sobs rack her body now. This was the first time she had said any of this out loud, the first time she'd had to truly explain her actions and her doubts and the holes in her memory. David had always counted on her, and this one time that he truly needed her, she'd let him down.

She may never be able to forgive herself for that, and now it seemed that possibly Ethan would not either.

Lucas simply sat quietly, waiting, letting her take whatever time she needed. After the memories of being harried and failing, begin given the space now was such a gift.

"That man at church this morning? The angry one I thought I heard say my name? That's David's younger brother, Ethan. He must have followed me out here to . . . punish me, or . . . I don't know. I couldn't bring myself to talk to him this morning, but I thought you should know."

"David's brother? You're sure?"

"Very. Of course, Ethan is missing his brother. I knew that," she said. "I didn't realize how much he blamed me for it though. Now that he's here, telling anyone who will listen, I vaguely remember whispers of questions at the funeral last year. Other people questioning what happened and what I could have done better. At the time—since then, in fact—I ignored all of it. I couldn't handle those accusations on top of my own guilt. But . . . it seems like they have all found me again."

Jenny felt as though a heavy quilt had been draped across her shoulders, pushing her down, keeping her down, drowning her in the past and the guilt. Pulling her hand away from Lucas, she put her head on her arms on the kitchen table and cried and cried.

———

Lucas felt his chest tighten—fear, anger, a whirl of emotions—as Jenny cried out her pain. Even after speaking to Jack that morning, he'd had doubts, but now Jenny's revelation had done away with all of that. He had not said a word while she explained the heavy secret she had carried all this way from Baltimore. While he did not know a thing about medicine, or even the kind of injuries being dragged through a street could cause, Lucas did not like the sound of Jenny's version of events. He would never accuse her of doing anything to another person intentionally, let alone her fiancé, but from what she said, it sounded as though she may have been negligent.

He did not know how to respond.

After another long moment, she raised her head, drying her eyes on the hand towel that she'd pulled out to dry the dishes.

"I'm sorry," she whispered. "I never thought any of this would follow me here. I don't know how to make up any of this to Ethan. Maybe it's not even possible to do so."

"That man claims that it is your fault his brother is dead?" Lucas asked in a low voice. He could not believe what he was hearing.

"I think so . . . I can't believe— The time and expense it must have taken him to come all the way to Wyoming! But . . . I suppose that's what finally showed me that I have been ignoring the enormity of what happened. I wanted to believe that it was my own personal tragedy, but I see now how blind that was."

"And you're sure that there's nothing more you could have done for David?"

Jenny looked at him, stricken and disbelieving. "Are you really asking me that?"

"I don't know what else to ask. Jenny, this is all new to me. I'm trying to be understanding but I just . . . I don't know."

"Lucas!"

Lucas ignored the guilt hammering at him for putting her in such a position, but he had to know. "You're a nurse, Jenny. You know better than I do how many different options and treatments there are. Didn't you just tell me that Teddy's injury reminded you of David's? And now he seems perfectly fine."

"Reminded me, yes, but it was far from as severe." She stood up and began pacing the floor. "I can't believe — How can you even—"

Suddenly, she stopped and whirled on him.

"You know what? You're right. You're right. I could not save David and given that there are big parts of that day that I can't even remember, who am I to say that I did everything I could do. Clearly Ethan has a reason to doubt me and . . . maybe he's right. Maybe it is my fault. And now you think so too."

She was barely getting the words out now; the sobs had returned. Lucas was torn between wanting to take her in his arms and comfort her and wanting to walk away from her for good. He did not know how to handle such news, especially from someone he had only just begun to trust. When Jack had relayed what this Ethan person had been saying, he had tried to forget it, the ravings of an angry stranger. But Jenny had all but confirmed every word.

This revelation changed everything between them.

She seemed to sense that, but he held himself back, stiffly wary of any movement she made toward him. This was the woman he trusted his daughter's health and well-being to and now he wasn't sure he knew her at all.

"I think it's best if we don't go back into town for a while," he said, trying to be firm but gentle. "Let this man calm down. Give you time to really think back to that day and see if there's anything else you remember, anything you regret not doing. I know that coming out here was supposed to be the new start for you, but some things we can't run from."

She looked at him with an anguished expression, though did not argue.

Without exchanging another word, he exited the kitchen, leaving her to her secrets.

CHAPTER SIXTEEN

Not only did Jenny not speak to Lucas at all the following day, but she didn't even see him. After she'd laid her heart bare, confessed her fears and her guilt, he had done nothing to reassure her. Nothing to bridge the growing chasm between them. Instead, he had only reinforced that it was possible she had done something truly unforgivable.

And then avoided her all day. He'd not shown up for breakfast, and had been closed in his office at supper.

She had hoped that by confessing her past, by opening herself up to his judgment and mercy, they might be drawn closer. That he might feel some kind of protectiveness over her. Truly, she would even take his pity at this point.

But she'd been naive, she realized as she kneaded a loaf of bread, pounding down with her mounting frustrations. Being vulnerable in front of Lucas had only served to make him more wary of her, and he'd rebuilt the icy wall between himself and the rest of the world. She had handed him the way to hurt her and now she did not know what to do.

Jenny had so been looking forward to her summer in Juniper Falls, to her future here with her new friends and chosen family. For the plans she and Mary had already talked about. For the gorgeous weather and landscape of the Great Plains. But now it seemed as though everything was pushing her away.

She went through the day in a hurt, frustrated distraction, at a complete loss for what she could do to fix any of it.

After going to bed early—the better to avoid Lucas —her sleep was disturbed several hours later by a pounding on the front door. She'd had trouble falling asleep, tossing and turning as her mind went over and over both what she'd said to Lucas and what memories she had from when David died. It felt like every time she circled around those memories they slipped away from her again. With everything that had happened—all the plans that had been put in jeopardy—Jenny had never felt so uncertain.

When the knock sounded on the front door of the ranch house, she woke immediately, jumping at the chance for a distraction. If she reached the door quickly enough, she could at least save others from being woken up.

After pulling a wrap around her, she stepped out into the hallway to see that Lucas had already reached the front door and was speaking urgently in a low voice to whoever was on the porch. She crept down the dark hallway, trying to overhear without being spotted. She wasn't sure she was ready to speak to Lucas yet.

. . . Rabbit holes . . . cattle hurt . . . not natural . . .

It sounded like Allan, but the little she heard was harried, sparse and enough to make Lucas panic. He was out the door without saying a word in response.

Jenny had a terrible feeling she could guess about what had happened. She returned to her room and dressed quickly. Thankful she wasn't venturing out into a thunderstorm in the middle of the night as she had before, Jenny stepped onto the front porch and looked around. In the distance toward the southwest, she noticed the bouncing light from lamps the men must be carrying, heading off to check whatever damage Allan had come to warn about.

Jenny looked the other direction.

It was pitch black, nearly midnight. A week past the full moon, there was still a good amount of light illuminating the ranch, casting deep shadows in all directions. Even so, she noticed a glimpse of movement, near to the gate that led to the road. At this distance, with so little light, there was no telling what that movement was, but Jenny had a terrible feeling about it.

Rather than going after Lucas and Allan to help them, Jenny trudged toward the movement she'd seen, keen to investigate. She clutched her coat tightly around her, the damp feel of a coming storm in the air.

The movement she was headed to grew more clear with every step she took. Soon Jenny was certain about the danger she was heading into. But someone had to. She could not walk away from this.

"Ethan Watts!" she called out when she got close enough. "What are you doing here? We're going to get the sheriff!"

The tall man, blond beard plain in the moonlight, sat on horseback, watching back down the road, back toward the stretch of pasture where Jenny knew Lucas and Allan to be. When he heard his name, Ethan startled, the horse underneath him jumpy as well.

"Can't prove anything," he grumbled at her, turning his horse toward town.

"Stop!" Jenny called, frantic, angry, confused. "How did you even find me? I asked you, what are you doing here?"

"Wasn't hard," he sneered at her. "You Sweet girls talk a lot. I admit it took me a few weeks, but I overheard your youngest sister mention Wyoming, and how far Juniper Falls was from a train station."

Jenny shook her head. "Ethan, really. Please don't do this. Let's talk. You can't just come after me—"

"Then," he continued loudly, as though she hadn't spoken, "turns out you just can't help but be in everybody's business, huh? Imagine my luck when I saw you bandaging some strange person's ankle that Saturday afternoon."

Jenny's heart leapt to her throat. "You were there?"

"How do you think I knew you'd be at church the next day?"

Jenny's mind was reeling. She still had trouble believing the lengths that Ethan would go to just to get to Wyoming, let alone every other step he'd taken to come after her, to punish her.

But perhaps that was her own short-sightedness.

As Jenny watched her late fiancé's brother seethe with fury, she realized anew that she had not been the only person so affected by David's death. He was so livid that his lashing out had now reached the other side of the continent. She pitied him—or would have if he were not so determined to ruin her life.

"You've not seen the last of me," he promised coldly. "I won't rest until everyone in this town—everyone in this *territory*—knows the damage you've wrought."

"Wait! Ethan!"

But calling after him was futile. She knew there was no way she could prove to the sheriff that Ethan was the one who had sabotaged the ranch, whatever Lucas was dealing with. And Ethan would never admit to it.

But more than seeing him brought to justice, what Jenny wanted most was to protect the ranch—and the people on it—from his destruction. She watched him ride swiftly away, back to Juniper Falls, and felt defeated. He was making problems for everyone.

———

When Allan had shown Lucas the hole in the pasture where one of the cattle had stepped and fractured its leg, he knew the ranch hand had been right. This was no simple rabbit hole; this had been dug deliberately, large enough and hidden with brush to ensure any one of his livestock could be injured if they stumbled across it. He'd tasked the two men with walking all over the acres looking for more holes that needed to be filled. They couldn't risk more accidents.

It was while walking slowly, quietly over the acres that Lucas heard Jenny yelling from somewhere else on the dark ranch. He had a time finding her—she had trekked out into the yard without any kind of lamp to light her way. When he reached her, she was looking down the dark, gravel road in the direction of town. Her arms were wrapped around her against the chill, shoulders slumped in defeat.

"What happened?" Lucas demanded, the first words he'd said to her in more than a day. "Are you all right?"

She turned in surprise at his voice, her expression betraying her relief at seeing him. Lucas knew that avoiding her all day had likely made Jenny feel something of rejection, but he'd needed to give himself time and space to determine how he felt about her confession.

Now, however, meeting on the dark road in the middle of the night, he felt unprepared for the comfort that she seemed to need from him in that moment.

"I'm all right," she assured him, despite her voice shaking.

Lucas watched the back of the man as he disappeared down the curve in the road. "Who was that? Did I hear you . . . ?"

He whirled on Jenny, eyes raking over her as he looked for any sign of her guilt or duplicitousness.

"Was that David's brother?"

"Ethan. Yes."

Though Lucas was not a man to kick someone when they were already down, he needed answers.

"Tell me," he demanded of her.

And so she did. About how she was woken by Allan coming to get him. About how she saw the movement and followed her instinct. About how she suspected he was the source of the problem the men were now dealing with. About how angry Ethan was with her, and how proud he was now to be causing her problems.

About how he'd promised to ruin her life.

By the end of her story, Jenny sounded numb, and he couldn't blame her. That was so much to deal with, on top of whatever worries she had about the ranch and likely a lack of sleep. But he hardened his heart against any pain she might be in. What was more clear to Lucas than ever was that he had been wrong to allow this woman to worm her way into his affection.

"I'm sorry," she was saying. "I had no idea he would . . . But I should have known. I should have done something. I don't know what, but . . ."

She was looking to him for reassurance. For answers. For someone to be on her team as she moved forward through this.

But that could not be him.

"You need to do something," he said in the businesslike tone he saved for official business with strangers. "It's to you to decide what, but *this* cannot continue."

"Of course. You're right. Maybe tomorrow we could—"

"No, Miss Sweet. There is no 'we' in this situation. Ethan Watts and his destruction is something that you brought to Prairie Winds Ranch, and something that *you* need to handle." He felt his anger rising as the full scope of the danger was made clear to him. "This man who is so erratic that he traveled across the continent for revenge found you, found *us*. He came here deliberately to cause us harm. Do you understand that?"

"I do. I'm—"

"I can't— I *can't* have this kind of danger around my home. My *daughter*."

"I'm so sorry," she sobbed out.

He sighed.

"I know you are. I do. I believe you that you did everything that you knew to do for David, and I know that it was never your intention to bring this kind of sabotage and anger to my doorstep, but the fact is it's here now. Ethan Watts is here in Juniper Falls and it sounds like he won't rest until he has ruined your life. I am sorry about that, but I can't let that ruin Mary's life too."

"I understand," she said softly, bowing her head against his frustrated words.

He felt a little guilty—he probably should not have yelled—but only a little bit. The truth was he was far more fearful for his daughter's safety than he was willing to let on. He had not been able to protect Mary from the heartbreak of losing her mother, and now it seemed he may not be able to protect her from the vindictiveness of this strange man.

"Figure it out," he said coldly, striding away from her back to the ranch house. He would check on his daughter. Make sure there was no other damage to the home than the holes dug in the pasture.

He felt a soft drop of rain on his shoulder, then another on his hat. The storm was coming in, chilling and destructive.

CHAPTER SEVENTEEN

The rain beat hard on her bedroom window as Jenny began packing her things to leave Prairie Winds Ranch and Wyoming all together.

She had been stung by Lucas's words, but even as he walked away from her, leaving her in the dark, on the road, as the rainstorm began, she could not blame him. Where she'd had the luxury of running away from her grief at David's death, Lucas had had to stay put, somehow managing through his grief as he raised his daughter. She could only imagine how difficult that entire situation had already been for him, and then she had gone and made it all worse by bringing this new danger to their doorstep. She could not judge his reaction now when it all came back to find her.

Though she'd been uncertain and frightened when Lucas had told her that she needed to be the one to handle this, she suddenly knew what she needed to do.

And so, she was packing.

And it was breaking her heart.

In the weeks that she'd lived at Prairie Winds Ranch, Jenny had quickly settled into her home here. Belongings were scattered all over her bedroom, and there were even some out into the living room and kitchen. She was trying to be thorough, even as she was determined to get everything packed before dawn.

Thankfully, the rest of the family was asleep as she tip-toed out to the common areas to collect her shawl, needlepoint, candleholders, and other doo-dads as quietly as she could. When she returned to her room, she shut the door silently and adjusted the wick of her oil lamp. She needed light. She needed to look plainly at her life, at her bedroom, at her things.

As she thought over all the mistakes that had led her to this difficult place, Jenny pulled out every item from the bottom of her trunk. It had long been in the family, and when he learned that she would be heading out to the territories, Jenny's father had insisted she take it.

"Your mother hoped you would see more than Baltimore," he had told her as they said goodbye. "I don't think this is what she had in mind, but I will pray for you every night, my dear."

That was one nice thing, Jenny thought as she piled her heavier items—books, boots—at the bottom of the trunk. Perhaps what she'd assumed to be her final farewell with her father would not be.

Next went in her clothing, her gowns, stockings, Bible, simple jewelry, framed watercolor of her childhood home that Eliza had painted years earlier. All the things that she brought to the ranch in an effort to make the place feel more like home as quickly as possible.

See how well that worked out, she scolded herself

silently. If she had not let herself open her heart so quickly, if she'd held herself at arm's length the way Lucas had, perhaps this retreat would not hurt as much.

Even if it took her until dawn, Jenny would face the new day ready to leave the ranch, ready to leave Juniper Falls. It was the only solution she could come up with to save those she cared about from further torment.

Though she wished that Lucas had not reacted the way he did to the news that Ethan had followed her out West, she could not blame him. There had been so much misfortune brought down on them in such a short period of time. Perhaps she was cursed. Things seemed to happen to her, all around her, and people who she loved got hurt. First her mother, then David, and now the whole family at Prairie Winds Ranch. For all she knew, she had saved her sisters from some heartbreak by leaving them behind.

And so, she would leave. That was the only option she had, now that Ethan had destroyed all the goodwill and connection she had created here in Juniper Falls. She would just have to admit defeat and return to Baltimore.

Jenny put the final bits in the top of her trunk, closed the lid, and sat on it. All the energy that had been driving her for the last couple of hours seemed to drain out completely. She felt overwhelmed with despondency to a level that she had not since David's death. Finding herself again after he was gone had been difficult, but she'd done it. She'd tried again. She'd accepted this position and uprooted her life and allowed herself to hope again.

And now it seemed that had been a mistake too.

Jenny Sweet was not sure she could stand changing her whole life a second time.

But then, what other choice did she have? Fortunately, she was well used to forcing herself through painful situations. If her time as a nurse had done anything, it was to give her the grit and backbone that many other people never reached.

While running away was cowardly, Jenny felt as though she had to do it.

Though she might not get a wink of sleep that night, she could still make things happen.

She made her plan. The sun would rise in just a couple hours. As soon as a hint of light peeked over the hills, she'd go find Teddy or Allan to take her to the train station. Or to take her to someone else who would drive her all the way to Laramie.

She would be gone before breakfast, out of the way, and out of Lucas's life forever.

———

The rain beat hard on his bedroom window as Lucas looked out over the ranch yard. His window faced behind the house, a view of the acres of grass where the cattle grazed, though he couldn't see much through the downpour. The weather, at least, matched his mood. Even though it was past midnight, he knew sleep was a long way from him.

When Allan had come to the front door of the ranch house to give him the bad news of the cow's injury and the suspicion of sabotage, he'd felt a fear that surprised him. He was used to being able to handle whatever came his way, but this dark attack, this slipping past him and coming after his herd, showed Lucas that he had left himself vulnerable.

When he'd seen who Jenny was speaking to at his front gate, when he'd realized what had happened, it had just about broken his heart. He didn't want to believe it. He didn't want to face what it meant that this woman was the reason that he and his home had become truly vulnerable for the first time ever.

This is what had come from letting down his guard—injury and destruction.

He paced to the other side of his bedroom and back again, willing the rain to clear so he could see something.

Willing his mind to clear so he would know what to do next.

Running his hands through his hair, Lucas looked around his room for his firearm. Something to help remind him that he was safe. That he had what he needed.

Though he did not regret what he'd said to Jenny—it had only been the truth—Lucas did regret that it had to be said. He had trusted her, and though that had proven to be a mistake, he would not further compound the mistake by letting this chink in his armor continue. He would always choose the safety of his daughter if that was at stake; he just wished there was some version of this where he did not have to make a choice.

He would never have believed that he could come to care for her so quickly, and yet here he stood in the middle of the night trying to justify some way to dismiss all the troubles that had driven a wedge between them.

He had never been much of a drinker, but he could

not deny that right now, with all this bearing down on him, a nip of whiskey might feel like a good escape. Instead, he made himself climb into bed. The covers up to his chin, Lucas closed his eyes, willing sleep to find him and release him from this worry, even if just for a few hours.

As he lay there, restless, Lucas did not see a way forward that he could be happy with. He had taken a big risk in inviting a new person into his life at all, let alone building a deeper friendship with her. Now it was clear that the risk was not going to pay off the way he'd hoped.

All he could think about was the fact that she would no longer be in his life. No one else had been able to reach past his cold walls since his wife's death, and now he would have to return to that same isolation. But what choice did he have?

She had brought the worst of her past to his front door.

He was still awake, and he was afraid to look at the clock to see how few hours remained before daylight. It would be a rough day; he would be tired and worried about Mary and scared for Jenny's welfare and having to make tough decisions.

The hardest part, he knew, would be breaking the news to Mary that her beloved Miss Sweet had to leave. He had no concerns about Mrs. Potter being willing to fill in the role until he found someone else, but it was clear after only a month or so that Jenny was far more to the little girl than just a caretaker. The day that they'd spent planting the vegetable garden together had made that clear.

But Mary had him, at least. That would never change.

Time passed, as it always did, albeit excruciatingly slowly. His eyes were still closed when he sensed the first dawn light coming through his windows.

CHAPTER EIGHTEEN

It was a sleepless several hours, but even after the darkest night, the sun will still rise. As the first part of her intention came together, Jenny was surprisingly clear-eyed despite not sleeping at all. She would get away from the Prairie Winds Ranch, protecting those she cared about, and would figure out the rest of her plan at some later time.

Leaving her trunk in the bedroom—the boys would have to bring it out to the wagon for her—Jenny tied on her bonnet, stepped out onto the porch, and took a deep breath of the morning air. The ground was still damp after the storm, but the sky was clear, indicating the start of a beautiful day on the plains. It would have broken Jenny's heart to miss the ranch on this spring day, if she had allowed herself to think about it.

But she didn't. There was no time for sentimentality. She wanted to get off the ranch before Lucas had even noticed she was leaving. She could not stand it if he had to ask her to go.

Although the ranch hands came into the kitchen for breakfast most mornings, Jenny was not sure where they might be this early, but she had some guesses. Milking the dairy cows Lucas kept was one of their first duties of the day, so Jenny trudged across the damp earth to the barn.

Inside the dim structure, Jenny immediately spotted Teddy sitting on a low stool behind one of the heifers. She didn't want to spook the animal, with the ranch hand's head so close to the rear hooves. Creeping closer, quietly, Jenny waited for him to notice her.

She cleared her throat.

"Miss Sweet?" he said, pausing in his work. "Is everything all right?"

"If you're just about done there," she said urgently, ignoring his question, "I need you. Please. Can you take a few hours and drive me to the train station? Or even drive me into Juniper Falls and I can hire a stagecoach? Something. Please help me get out of here. I can't stay."

"Miss Sweet?" The poor boy looked utterly bewildered.

"Please," she insisted. "I'll pay. Whatever you think is fair. And a big tip if you can get my trunk on the same train as me, as well."

"I can't just leave the ranch. I'm sorry. Let me talk to Mr. Garrett."

"No! No, this needs to be done without him. It's what he wants."

"He didn't say anything to me about it . . . No, Miss Sweet, I'm sorry."

To his credit, he did look sorry. Teddy was always the kind of young man who wanted to help whenever he could. But Jenny also knew that if he agreed to take her, he would be dooming himself to questions or trouble when he returned.

"Not even to Juniper Falls?" she asked desperately.

"Where are you going?" a small voice asked.

Jenny looked back to see little Mary lurking by the door to the barn, her well-loved doll clutched to her chest.

"Sweetheart, what are you doing here? Did you come looking for me?"

It was so early, and she had never seen Mary in the barn without her father. She could only assume that the little girl had heard some of her pacing, heard her slip out the door that morning and been upset by it. The poor child looked very worried.

Though she had not admitted it to herself, she'd been hoping she could slip out without seeing the little girl. She was not prepared for a difficult goodbye with this child who had already lost her mother and whose father had been distant for years. She would just be one more adult who was leaving her. Jenny swallowed hard. She'd come to treasure this little girl in the weeks since she'd arrived in Wyoming and now felt a wave of guilt at leaving her.

"Miss Sweet, where are you going?" Mary prodded, worry now clear in her tone.

"You must be cold, sweetheart. Where is your hat? Have you eaten breakfast? I think Mrs. Potter is in the kitchen. Let's get you in there."

"I heard you talking out here." She peered past Jenny to where Teddy stood awkwardly after trying to extricate himself from the conversation. "Are you leaving?"

"I think I have to. There's a lot going on and I just think it will be better for everyone if I'm not here anymore."

"But . . . But . . . You're leaving *me?*" Mary asked again, lip trembling.

"Let's go out to the sunshine, pet," she said, leading the girl out of the barn.

It broke Jenny's heart to hear such pain in the little girl's voice. This was precisely why she'd come out here first thing in the morning—she didn't want to make a scene, she didn't want anyone to try to stop her. The last thing she wanted to do was hurt Mary, but neither did she want to lie to her.

Once they were out in the yard, in the sunshine, Jenny squatted down in front of Mary so the two were eye to eye. It was at that moment that she noticed how green the child's eyes were. How big and trusting.

"I have to go. I'm so sorry to be leaving you, but I am so glad that I got the chance to meet you, my dear girl."

She offered her hand, palm up. Mary looked down at it, then up at Jenny's face. She seemed to be warring with herself whether or not to take Jenny's hand, but after a few moments, gently set her tiny fingers in Jenny's palm.

The little girl's soft, warm hand was so trusting, so delicate, Jenny was reminded all over again what she'd be leaving behind if she returned to Baltimore. But she saw no alternative, really, since her troubles had followed her out here to the frontier.

"There are things that might happen if I stay," Jenny continued cautiously. "Things that I don't want to happen, that might not happen if I leave."

"But— But other bad things might happen if you

leave," Mary said, edging on panic. "You belong here. Just tell my papa. He'll make sure that nothing happens here."

"Oh!" Jenny pushed down a sob. "I know this might be difficult to understand, but there are things even grown-ups can't stop from happening, sweetheart. Even a man as strong and good as your papa."

"But— You can't leave! We need you. Who is going to garden with me if you leave? Or make my new dress? Please? I love you."

Mary was all but wailing now, trying to throw herself into Jenny's arms with the desperation of a child who could not picture her life any differently. With the little girl's arms wrapped around Jenny, she tried to soothe her, tried to quiet her. Tried to think about what to say to reassure Mary.

But the only thing that came to mind was to remind the child that her own mother had left and she'd been all right afterwards.

What kind of thing would that be to say to a little girl? A little girl who so clearly adored her, despite her faults or imperfections.

And what kind of person would she be if she abandoned this sweet child, knowing what it would mean for her.

There had only been one other time in her life that Jenny had run away from a situation—when David had died and she'd ended up here in Wyoming. She could not do that again. She did not want to become the kind of person who simply retreated from problems. David had never done that as a doctor; she had never done that with her sisters, with losing her mother, with difficult nursing assignments, or with any other obstacle that had come up.

Jenny had always fought for what was right before.

She took a deep breath, making her decision. She would stay, fight for what was right. Though she might not be able to convince Ethan to leave her alone, if she did not at least *try*, she would never feel worthy of Mary's love.

Of Lucas's, if it came to that.

"All right," she murmured. "It's okay. I won't go. I'll stay here with you."

Mary clung tighter to Jenny's neck.

"Sweetheart," she said gently. "I need you to let go of me, please. I need to take care of something before your papa wakes up. I'm not leaving."

Mary pulled away and wiped her running nose on the sleeve of her nightdress. "You're not leaving?"

"I need to go into town, but I'll be back." She looked directly into the little girl's eyes, well aware of the sanctity of a vow made to a child. "I promise I'll be back later today. Why don't you go inside and ask Mrs. Potter to help you get dressed? You'll need to wash the mud off your feet. And tell her I'll be back as soon as I can. Can you do that for me? Be strong and patient and take care of your papa while I'm gone?"

Mary nodded her head.

"All right. Go on now."

When the child ran to the house, Jenny turned back to Teddy, who had ventured out of the barn.

"I still need you to take me into town, though," she said in a low voice to him. "I won't be long. There's just something I need to do."

———

Lucas had not slept well that night; his dithering over what to do about Jenny had kept his mind racing. And so before dawn, he gave up trying to sleep much and rose to make himself some coffee. While that brewed, he went into his office with an idea to look for the letters that he and Jenny had exchanged. Perhaps she had told him some hint of this and it was his own lack of attention that had set his expectations wrong. He wanted to do anything he could to make sure she was not taking on his own guilt and failure.

From the window in his office that looked out onto the porch, Lucas could see Jenny speaking urgently to Teddy just inside the barn doors. He could not hear what was being said from this distance, but she seemed agitated; he seemed reluctant. He'd almost turned away when he saw his own little girl running down the porch steps through the mud to Jenny. She seemed to try to soothe Mary as the latter threw herself into her arms adoringly.

There was more conversation, nodding, and assurances—Lucas wished he could hear what was being said —before Mary ran back inside.

After their conversation on Sunday where she had laid bare the truth, Lucas did not know what to think about any of it. While Jenny had every right to keep her past private, to mourn her late fiancé as she saw fit, he'd agonized over what that meant for his daughter, for his home.

But now, seeing the way that Mary clung to Jenny's

neck as though being saved from drowning, he realized there must be another side to the entire situation.

Maybe she had made mistakes. Maybe she had not handled past situations as well as a person might hope, but he knew her. If Lucas was certain of anything, it was that Jenny Sweet always did her best—learning as she went if necessary, but she tried.

Who was he to reject her for something out of her control?

He was about to go talk to her when through the office window the scene shifted. As Lucas watched, Teddy brought the wagon around and helped Miss Sweet into it, then drove off toward the road. This early in the morning, where could she be going but the train station?

He couldn't let her go. He had to apologize, tell her they would figure it out together.

The coffee boiled over and Lucas hurried to take it off the fire. There was no time to drink it if he wanted to stop Jenny from leaving.

Lucas dressed as quickly as he could before saddling Bo and following after his wagon.

CHAPTER NINETEEN

"You sure you don't want me to go in there with you?" Teddy asked her, looking worriedly to the front door of the General Sherman Inn.

At Jenny's insistence, he had driven her into Juniper Falls as quickly as he could, though they were somewhat hampered by the muddy road. They had reached Juniper Falls in the middle of a busy morning—so busy that at first, Teddy had trouble finding a spot to stop the wagon so she could get out. Though she had spent the entire drive into town thinking about what she wanted to say to Ethan, now that she was here her mind seemed empty. But she couldn't go back yet. She was determined to stand up for what was right and good in her life, defending her chosen family at Prairie Winds Ranch however she could.

She was afraid that after his antics of the night before, Ethan Watts might be trying to leave town too. Though she did not know precisely where to find him, the hotel in the center of town seemed like the most logical place to start.

Jenny shook her head, determined. "Thank you, Teddy, but this is something I need to do for myself. If I don't, he'll never leave me alone." She looked him in the eye. "He'll never leave *us* alone. We can't risk having him think he can just come back to the ranch any time to harass me. Besides, it's the middle of the morning in the middle of town. What could he do to me?"

"I've seen what some men can do," Teddy murmured. "But I'll be right out here. If I hear you yelling, I'm coming in anyway, no matter what you say."

"I understand. You're a good man, Teddy." She put a comforting hand on his forearm.

"Yes, ma'am," he said, blushing.

Jenny climbed down from the wagon and readied herself to confront Ethan. If he wasn't here, she'd try the boarding house. If he wasn't there, maybe the saloon. Maybe the cafe. Maybe the train station. If all else failed, she could ask someone; she had a suspicion that his brash complaining had made it so many folks in Juniper Falls might know where to find him, if only so they could avoid him. If she didn't find him before he left town, she would spend the rest of her life looking over her shoulder, wondering when he would show up again to try to ruin her life.

For Mary, for Lucas. For all the people in Juniper Falls that she cared about, Jenny needed to take care of this situation now.

She took a deep breath, steeled herself, and stepped through the wide wooden front doors of the General Sherman Inn. It was all polished wood inside, including a substantial staircase leading to the upper floors, but she didn't have the mind to look around. There was no one at the front desk, but to the left of the door was a sitting area and she spotted two men lounging in front of the big fireplace in the lobby. The taller of the two stood when he noticed her.

Ethan looked like he had been drinking for months, his beard stained with tobacco juice. Despite her frustration, Jenny's heart went out to him. He was grieving David just as deeply as she was, and handling it far worse.

He took a couple steps toward her. "You come to break my arm too? Maybe poison? Suffocation?"

"What on earth are you talking about?"

Whatever Jenny had expected from Ethan, she had underestimated the vitriol. It was clear from this greeting that he despised her, assuming the very worst.

They had been friendly once, Jenny and Ethan. He was the same age as her, three years younger than David, and had always been a good comrade in the time that she'd spent with the Watts family. After David had died, he'd shut her out, shut everyone out of his life as he mourned his brother and his best friend. At the time, Jenny had thought perhaps they might exchange a letter or two to keep in touch, but she was too sad about David to give the rest of his family much thought.

Now, however, she could see that there was a long road, possibly insurmountable, between whatever Ethan was feeling and the chance that they could even be polite to each other again. She had taken steps to heal her heart, while he had wallowed in his pain and blamed her for every ounce of it.

"Is that what you really think of me?" she asked calmly. "That I'm that violent and destructive? Ethan . . ."

"What else am I supposed to think? My brother was walking with you and then something happened and in just a few minutes he was dead, and you had done *nothing*, walking away with just a bruise or two."

She sighed. He was so deep in his grief, she wasn't sure there was any way to get through to him. All around her, the lobby had begun to fill up with workers, other guests, maybe even strangers off the street who had been drawn by his shouting. But she did not take her eyes off Ethan. This was her one chance to stand up to him, to not run again. If she let him harass her further, he would never stop.

This was between her and him.

"You can't do this anymore. I won't allow it. You're nothing but a bully, Ethan. You're hurting and you want everyone else to hurt too."

"Everyone should hurt! You especially."

He took another step toward her, but Jenny braced herself to avoid shying away.

"I know how badly you want to make this my fault. You want to make it anyone else's fault so you have someone to be angry at. But the truth is sometimes accidents just happen. Those horses got spooked. Their driver did his best to rein them in. Frankly, we should be grateful that no one else got hurt. The bystanders all tried to help as best they knew how."

"But it wasn't enough!" he yelled.

"No." Jenny felt that heartbreak of losing David all over again. "No, it wasn't enough. But . . . sometimes difficult things happen, and it's our job to make the best of the resulting situation. Can you even imagine what David would think if he knew what you were doing to me? *Our* David, who regularly had to tell husbands that their wife had passed or mothers that their child may not live to see adulthood? David knew what it was like to try and fail. He would not have held me to this impossible standard that you are."

"He's not *your* David," he seethed.

"Honestly, Ethan, I don't need you to believe me. I know that I did my best, whether you do or not. I've come to terms with the fact that even my best wasn't enough, as much as that breaks my heart. I loved your brother. I was looking forward to spending the rest of my life with your brother. I lost just as much as you did when he died. More probably. I mourn that day constantly, and I'm not going to let you make it any worse for me."

"Well that's too bad, because I aim to make every day the worst for you if I can."

"Ethan . . ." she pleaded.

Jenny did not know what else she could say to get through to this man. He simply had too much hate and vindictiveness in his heart. While she did believe she had done her best for David, her own sorrow at his death and recognizing Ethan's made it difficult for her to hold firm in that belief. She had cared about Ethan, had once valued his opinion of her.

That was just one more thing she had to put behind her now.

"I'm not done with you," he said, far more coldly than Jenny would have predicted. "I'm not going to rest until I up-end your life the way you did mine. We'll just see who is going to suffer more."

He walked so closely to her on his way to the front door of the inn that Jenny thought he might run right into her. His tall frame towered over her, Ethan putting all his effort into intimidating her. Though Jenny's hands were shaking, she did not cower away; she met his eyes and held his gaze until he turned away to exit.

All around her a quiet murmuring hummed while Jenny sunk into one of the chairs by the fireplace.

———

Lucas spotted Teddy waiting in his wagon in front of the inn and directed Bo to his side.

"She in there?" he asked simply.

"Boss! You scared me." Teddy had guilt written all over his expression.

"Didn't expect me to find out about this?"

"No, I guessed you might. Just, maybe, you know, when we got back to the ranch."

"Did she come after Watts?"

Teddy nodded. "I think so. I offered to go in with her, but . . ."

"It's fine, Ted. I don't blame you at all. That woman could build a house with just her two hands if she had a mind to. We'll make sure she stays safe, but this is her fight."

"Yes, sir."

He tossed Bo's reins to Teddy, trusting the ranch hand to take care of the animals in the interim. While he had no intention of getting in the way of whatever

Jenny was doing, he could not just sit by and wait. Even if—*especially* if—she didn't know he was in there, Lucas wanted to be on hand just in case the whole thing went south.

He could hear the shouting from out on the board-walk, and it only got louder when he opened the door and entered the inn. A small crowd was starting to gather, curious onlookers from elsewhere in the hotel and passersby from outside like himself.

Jenny was standing proudly in the middle of the room, looking up at the unkempt stranger who was loudly raving at her. Lucas took in her chin, bravely lifted, the hurt in her eyes as she absorbed the abuse. He wanted so badly to sail in and teach this man a lesson, but he also knew she might not forgive him for meddling.

It had to be enough that he was here, just in case.

"I loved your brother," she was saying when he entered. "I was looking forward to spending the rest of my life with your brother. I lost just as much as you did when he died . . ."

Lucas looked around the lobby of the inn, marveling at how many folks were unabashedly listening in on this argument. Poor Jenny would never have dreamed that she'd lay her heart bare in front of so many strangers. Even as she stood up to her bully, she looked exhilarated, though exhausted. Lucas had to fight his urge to take her in his arms and relieve her of every burden, every worry.

Soon, Ethan reached the end of his rope and pushed past Jenny, pushed through the crowd and out the front door of the inn. Lucas had half a mind to go after him, but focused on the real reason he had come into town.

Jenny sunk into one of the chairs and leaned forward, resting her head in her hands.

Lucas's heart went out to her. He swiftly crossed the room and crouched down in front of her, warning off anyone else who looked like they might want to approach.

"Are you all right?" he asked softly.

She looked up and gasped in surprise. "Lucas! What are you doing here?"

"I saw you leave with Teddy and came after you. I wasn't sure what you would be doing, but I couldn't let you take on too much."

"You did?"

"Just in case." He grinned. "I see that I didn't need to worry about you at all."

"I'm not sure about that. It's not as though I chased Ethan to a train. He claims he's not done with me."

"We can worry about that if it happens. Let's not go borrowing trouble."

"I don't know how I got through that. I was shaking the whole time, but . . . I thought about what you said."

"About . . . About how I couldn't have that kind of danger around my daughter? I'm sorry, I shouldn't have—"

"Yes, you should. Really. That made it very clear to me what was at stake in all of this and helped me realize that I only had two options."

He held her gaze for a long moment, understanding without words what was left unsaid.

"But you stayed," he said softly.

She shrugged, a little embarrassed. "Well, I had to

stand up to a bully first, but yes, I thought I would stay in Juniper Falls. If that's all right with you."

"Of course it is. I'm so grateful. I don't know what Mary would do without you."

As soon as the words were out of his mouth, Lucas realized there was something else he wanted to say, more things he could say. But now was not the time.

"Let's get back to the ranch," he continued. "Let that man stew in his own fury and make Mary's day by showing her you've returned."

CHAPTER TWENTY

After Ethan left her behind and stormed out of the inn, Jenny felt marginally better. She had stood up to him, not letting his height and his anger and his violence intimidate her, doing what she knew to be right despite it all. She knew it likely would not be the last time, and she would do the same thing again if she had to, as many times as it took. She was far from sure that the confrontation would do any good. There might be no way to reach the Ethan who she used to be friends with.

The only thing she could do was look forward to the next step—returning to her duties at Prairie Winds Ranch, with Mary, with Lucas, with the whole family. She wanted to focus on building this new life to be exactly what she wanted.

After sending Teddy on ahead with Bo, Jenny and Lucas rode back to the ranch together in the wagon. She found herself stealing glances at his strong profile more than once on the silent drive, though she was hesitant to speak. The last conversation they'd had was about how much her presence was a detriment to the ranch.

But . . . his coming into town gave her a small bit of hope that he had forgiven her for the mess she'd dragged them into.

"Thank you for coming after me," she said softly.

"Mm-hmm," he said simply.

Jenny wanted him to say more. She was unsure where they currently stood, but she decided it was best not to ask too many questions.

With Ethan's vows to make her pay fresh in her memory, she felt as though there could be a snake around any corner. That man knew where she was. He knew where the ranch was. Though she was grateful that Lucas was not forcing her to leave, Jenny wondered how difficult a situation they were going to find themselves in.

The spring season was upon them, and this drive was very different from their silent travel from the Laramie train station a few weeks earlier. Now, instead of muddy and gray landscape, everywhere Jenny looked were signs of new life. Hope. Tall grass was bravely shooting up all across the rolling hills, and in the wide-open spaces where no cattle grazed, she even noticed splotches of color—purple, yellow, orange wildflowers creating an enticing palette. The view made her wish she could share this with her sisters.

If things ever settled down around here.

As they drew closer to the ranch, she felt cautiously optimistic. There was still every chance Lucas might decide that keeping Jenny at the ranch was too much of a risk. Ethan might not leave her alone, but she believed now that Lucas would at least try to help her get rid of him.

She no longer felt completely alone in her struggles.

She glanced at him again, noting his broad shoulders as he sat proudly, driving the team back to his ranch. His small empire that he had poured so much work and love into. She was proud to be by his side as he built this home for his daughter, and hoped that she could do him, Mary, and Prairie Winds Ranch justice.

She realized—sitting there next to Lucas grateful for the support and confidence he had shown in her—that there was nothing she wanted more than for Prairie Winds Ranch to be her home. For Lucas, Mary, and even Mrs. Potter and the ranch hands to be her family. She felt a soothing comfort here that could not be replaced, and she wanted to spend the rest of her life at Lucas's side.

Her heart started pounding as she realized what that meant.

Jenny looked away from him, down at her hands clasped in her lap, for fear her feelings would be plain on her face.

She loved him. She knew that now. She wanted this life *with* him, if only Ethan didn't ruin everything.

Maybe it would come to nothing. Maybe they would simply work side by side.

It was enough—for now—that she didn't have to leave this place after all the work she'd done to make a home here.

They reached the ranch just after mid-day.

"Is there anything you need from me before supper?" he asked as he helped her down from the wagon.

"Oh, um . . . no. No, I don't think so." She wasn't ready to admit that she had not planned to even be there that day, so any thoughts of what needed to be done had completely flown from her mind. She realized that, though Mrs. Potter had likely seen to Mary and feeding the ranch hands, there would still be plenty to do. Including unpacking her trunk.

"All right then. I'll be around if you change your mind. I'm glad you're back," he said simply before tipping his hat and leading the horses to the barn.

Jenny did not know how to respond. She, too, was glad to be back, even if the events of the previous twenty-four hours had done damage to the cautious friendship the two of them were building. She hoped they could return to their previous intimacy.

She loved him. She wanted so much more, but if they could get back what they had, she would try to be satisfied.

For now, though, her duty was clear. Take care of the house. Take care of the child. Be a support to the rancher as much as she could. He owed her nothing beyond the wages and room and board in their contract.

————

When Lucas left Jenny at the house and went looking for the ranch hands, it was not because he had any particular need of them. It was because he did not know what to say to her. The silent drive back to the ranch gave him plenty of time to think over the situation with Ethan and he was far from coming to any conclusions.

What she had done was admirable. It must have

been so frightening for her to confront that man at all, let alone confront him in such a public place. There was no doubt that stories of their confrontation would be all over Juniper Falls before nightfall. The folks who had only just met Jenny would now know all of her business.

Lucas realized that it would be his responsibility to help protect her reputation. Allowing her to stay at the ranch, despite the trouble on their doorstep, was just one part of publicly supporting her. Maybe he should have one of the boys go into town, or even Mrs. Potter, to keep an ear out and make sure the rumors did not get worse.

Lucas knew that gossip spread through a small town like wildfire, but beyond that, he didn't feel prepared for what Ethan Watts had brought to his life.

He led the horses into the barn, still hitched to the wagon, deep in his own thoughts. The ranch hands were repairing some of the gardening tools in advance of the spring growing season, but Teddy stopped and stood up when he saw Lucas.

"What happened in town?" Allan asked. "Did you bring Miss Sweet back with you?"

Lucas looked from one ranch hand to the other. "You boys been gossiping while I was gone?"

"No, sir," Teddy answered. "I was just worried. We were. You know she came to me before breakfast and asked me to drive her to the train station?"

Lucas busied himself unhitching Lacey from the wagon. "I suspected something like that. No, she came home with me. She'll settle in just fine now, I hope. Gave that Watts man a piece of her mind, too. Dunno if it will make any difference, but it probably made her feel better. We should try to be especially kind to her today."

"Watts is the one that dug the holes to injure the cattle?"

"That's right. We think so, at least. It's not my story to tell, but I will say this. Miss Sweet is doing her best, and she deserves whatever help and protection from this man we can give, all right? So if you see him around here again, you have my permission to drive him off with force if necessary."

"Yes, sir," Allan said somberly. "Miss Sweet has always been good to us, kind and understanding and generous. I can't imagine there's anything she could've done to deserve what that man is trying to do to her."

"That's right!" Teddy added excitedly. "Me too! Why, she was right on hand to help when I got that fence rail right through me."

"You didn't get it through you," Allan pointed out calmly.

"And then when we got to town," Teddy continued, ignoring his friend, "she knew that fella was gonna yell and rave at her and she still walked right into the inn with her head held high. I think I heard her say she's had some sorrow in her past, but she deserves something better than that."

"She does," Lucas agreed. "Thank you, boys. I surely do appreciate your concern for her. And I know Miss Sweet will too."

He left them to their work and made his way around the outside of the barn to the big bur oak—his favorite place when he needed solitude. It was where he went the morning after Christine had died and he had to face a life, and raise their daughter, without her. It was where he went the morning after they had moved to the ranch, when he was doubting that they would be able to make it out here in a frontier town away from their families.

Every time that Lucas had to give himself a talking to, he found that the best place to do so was the quiet stillness under the bur oak. The broad trunk reminded him how old the tree was, that it had been there long before him and likely would stay long after him. It helped put his own problems into perspective.

Listening to Teddy and Allan talk about how much they admired Jenny had fanned a flame inside him that he had been deliberately stifling. He still saw himself as the broken, cold man who had been widowed and left with a small child, but over the last month or so since her arrival, he had felt himself more and more in the sunshine.

Lucas realized he had laughed more since Jenny moved in than he had in years. He had spent more deliberate time with Mary than he had in years. He had even enjoyed the afternoon picnic the previous Saturday more than any other town excursion he could remember.

And what was the common thread?

Jenny Sweet.

Lucas sunk to the grass at the foot of the oak tree and leaned back to look up into the branches, winding and twisting and curving down toward him.

It wasn't so much of a bolt from the blue as it was the slow realization of something that had been there all along, like when a flower that wasn't there the day before is suddenly in full bloom and a foot tall.

He loved Jenny Sweet.

He could not hide from that realization now.

When he had been so upset by Ethan coming to sabotage the ranch, it was a fury that simply protected him from the fact that he loved Jenny and could not stand to see her in danger. She had made every part of his life better—most importantly his relationship with his daughter. He could not do without her any more than he could do without food in his belly or air in his lungs.

Recognizing this truth both changed everything for Lucas, and nothing. He would still defend Jenny against Ethan. Still want to spend every day working alongside her.

But what did she want? Could she possibly love him back?

Lucas sank back against the oak's trunk and thought about his next steps.

CHAPTER TWENTY-ONE

Jenny sat back on her heels and wiped as much dirt off her hands onto her apron as she could. Though she would never admit it, there was something very satisfying about seeing narrow crescents of dirt wedged under her fingernails. It spoke to the reward of accomplishment; she was secretly thrilled that this evidence of her own handiwork would likely carry through the rest of her day, no matter how vigorously she washed her hands.

Working in the dirt like this also reminded her of one of her most special memories with Lucas. The day that she had spent in the garden with him tilling the earth had been the first time they had really been open with each other, and when she had let him see some of her past. Her heartbreak. It was as though turning over the soil had helped her turn over a new leaf in her own life. Resetting. Starting again.

And that new beginning had brought her to this moment, to carefully weeding around the tiny beginnings of new life that she was nurturing, while also care-fully protecting her heart and the realization of her new love.

The day they had spent with Mary was also special—planting all of these fruit and vegetables for the family's future had been a gracious, promising delight. The easy nature with which all three of them interacted—like a family—while working together to put the tiniest seeds in the ground felt more natural to Jenny than just about anything else ever had. Even when she'd been working hard at the hospital, coming home to her sisters, it had felt like a choice she had to make every day. Though she loved the work, loved helping people, she also woke up every morning with a small amount of dread. Whose death would she witness that day? Whose heart would she have to break with bad news? Knowing that her occupation was for the greatest good of the community kept her going, but there were nights when she came home from her shift and went straight to bed without even saying hello to her sisters.

It had been fulfilling but difficult.

This—the fresh air, the growing things, the frontier opportunity—was far better.

This life on Prairie Winds Ranch now felt as natural as breathing to her. She knew she would see the clear benefit of her labor when the strawberry plant sprouts broke ground and Mary's excitement could not be contained. She could already tell how much better she was making Mrs. Potter's golden years by letting her stay off her feet.

She could see the difference in the way Lucas carried himself, less withdrawn and prickly, though she was not quite confident enough to attribute those changes to her presence.

Jenny found so much satisfaction in this ranch life; there seemed to be almost nothing that could be improved.

Almost, her heart whispered.

It had been a few days now since she had confronted Ethan in Juniper Falls and, while the fact that they hadn't heard anything more from him was positive, she had a feeling it wasn't over. Ethan was too stubborn to disappear after just a relatively small confrontation. As much as Jenny reveled in the peace and serenity of life on the ranch, she treasured it enough to not take it for granted.

And so, on this late afternoon as she tended to the blossoming garden, she was as content as a person could be. This was all what she'd wanted.

"It looks wonderful."

Jenny turned to see Lucas coming across the yard to where she knelt by the garden. The sun was sinking low in the sky, and while in the back of her mind she realized she should be starting supper, at that moment all she could think about was how handsome he looked, striding across the verdant land with the sunset behind him.

"Thank you! I had some help," she said as he approached.

———

Lucas had been watching Jenny work in the garden for several minutes before he made his presence known.

One of the things that he'd admired most about her since she'd arrived was the way that she had no hesitation about getting her hands dirty in the service of her task. Though he assumed it was a characteristic she'd developed in her work as a nurse—he could not fathom how much blood and such she'd seen every day—it was precisely the kind of thing that a woman living on the frontier needed.

It was further proof that this was the woman for him, this was the life for him.

As soon as Jenny had arrived, she'd dived headfirst into any task that was needed to make this place a home, a working ranch, a safe haven for his daughter, and he could not even begin to express his gratitude to her for all that she had given his family.

He wanted to try, though.

When he saw that she was taking a break from her weeding and pruning, sitting back on her heels to admire her work, he took the chance to join her.

"It looks wonderful," he called.

She looked up at him, and the peace he noticed in her face as he walked toward her was comforting. She seemed so happy, and only more so when she saw him coming. The sun was setting behind him, the warm, pinkish late afternoon light illuminating her whole being, reminding him forcefully of light from Heaven coming down to mark God's favorites.

"I had some help," she called back.

"Do you need more now?" he asked as he reached her.

"Oh . . ." She looked around at her work, as though deciding something. "Not today. This is the kind of project that will never be done. There will be plenty more chances for you to help take care of everything."

She climbed to her feet but lost her balance briefly, her ankle turning on the uneven ground. Lucas stretched out to steady her, catching her with a hand on her waist and one on her forearm. His heart began pounding at Jenny's hands on his shoulders.

"Oh!" she gasped, looking up at him.

There was a long moment, the air crackling between them, before she looked away.

"I'm so clumsy. Thank you."

But even as she stepped out his embrace, he caught her hand in his.

"Wait," he said, his voice husky. "Please. I've been thinking about other chances for me to . . . help take care of everything."

Jenny blushed, but did not look away, did not withdraw her hand from his.

"I don't know where to start," he admitted.

Jenny took a tiny half-step toward him, and he took that opportunity to catch her other hand. He held both now as her sweet, trusting face looked up at him, giving him the quiet and space to take the time he needed. It was just further confirmation that this woman knew him deeply.

"I know that I've closed myself off from the rest of the world," he said. "After what I went through and what I had to give up, I've been afraid to let anyone else get close."

"You?" she teased, gently. "Lucas Garrett, fearless when climbing on top of the barn in the middle of a thunderstorm, isn't afraid of anything."

"Broken limbs can heal. Broken hearts . . ."

He left the end of his sentence unfinished. If anyone knew what a person with a broken heart had to go through, it was her. She nodded, silently nudging him to continue.

"Until I met you, I didn't know what I was missing. I didn't realize how much Mary was missing. It took a complete stranger coming into our lives to show us how much better things could be. I have been punishing myself for my late wife's death, and it took seeing you put yourself through the same for me to learn that that is not the way forward.

"Jenny, you have become the best part of my life. Of Mary's life. I truly don't know what the ranch or our family would do without you. All I know is I never want to let you go."

"Lucas . . ." she said, through happy tears.

"I love you," he said, unable to take his eyes off her.

He held his breath, waiting for her response, praying she could see past the cold man he had been to what was now in his heart.

"I . . . am overwhelmed," she said, finally. "I didn't expect any of this. I didn't let myself even hope to find anyone at this stage of my life, and I showed up here, and you . . . Mary and all of it . . ." She laughed at herself, even as a happy tear trailed down her cheek. "I don't have any words for what I am feeling other than I love you too. This is all more than I could have dreamed of."

He brought her hands to his lips, kissing her still-dirty knuckles reverently.

"I'm sorry about—"

"No, no." He stopped her. "No apologies. I heard

what you said in the inn's lobby. I believe you have only ever done your best and there is absolutely nothing to apologize for. And if you'll have me, I intend to make sure that you live the rest of your life knowing that."

"Really?" she asked.

"I love you, Jenny Sweet. My daughter loves you. I want to marry you. I want to spend the rest of my life taking care of you. Please say that you will join our family, that you will be my wife and my heart and my bond."

She had tears in her eyes even as she beamed at him, and Lucas reflected that her willingness to wear her emotions on her sleeve was just one more way she would be an irreplaceable influence on him and Mary as they built their life together.

"I can't wait," she said.

In that moment, every mistake Lucas had ever made seemed forgiven. The world felt right in a way that it had perhaps never felt before. Without losing a single second more, Lucas leaned down to his bride-to-be, sealing their betrothal with a kiss.

CHAPTER TWENTY-TWO

In spite of everything—the hard journey out to Wyoming, Lucas's initial gruffness, the harassment by Ethan—Jenny was not sure she had ever in her life been happier. Hearing Lucas say that he loved her was beyond even her wildest dreams. This was a man who loved hard and who took great pride in caring for the people that he loved. There was no doubt in her mind that with him by her side, she could get through whatever this trial with Ethan would be. It might not happen immediately, but she knew they could build a life together.

After the romantic sanctity of his confession and proposal, the pair did an even more loving thing and went inside to make supper together. It was prosaic but somehow that made it more special. This was not a love that only blossomed at the edges, the special circumstances, and hard-won moments. If the last weeks had taught Jenny anything, it was that their bond would grow even stronger with the day-to-day tasks and work and building. They could lean on each other and choose love every day.

Though he had not cooked for years, Lucas did not want to leave her side, and so Jenny put him to work peeling potatoes. Working side by side like this was just as soothing as it had been when fixing the barn stalls and tilling the garden. With Lucas as her teammate, Jenny had every faith that their life would be very happy together.

She had just filled a pot full of water to make soup when Allan entered the kitchen, looking between them cautiously.

"Don't worry," she said, teasingly. "I won't put you to work too."

"Do you need—?

"No, really," Jenny said. "What can we do for you? Supper in a few hours."

She dropped the remains of last night's roasted chicken into the water and put it over a low flame before turning back to her cutting board to start slicing an onion.

———

Lucas noticed the expression on Allan's face and set the half-peeled potato down to give him his full attention.

"Boss," Allan said in a low voice. "Can I talk to you?"

"Sure thing. Go ahead."

The ranch hand glanced at Jenny and then back to Lucas with a meaningful expression. "No, sir, I can wait until you're not busy."

Lucas shook his head. "You can say whatever you

need to say now. I assure you, Miss Sweet doesn't mind. She's part of this family too and you know how I feel about secrets. Nothing can improve or be fixed if we don't know about it."

"I really don't," she said kindly. "Don't mind me at all."

Allan took a deep breath, and Lucas could tell from his face that he was considering his next words carefully.

"It's just that, sir, me and Teddy just got back from town . . ."

"Mm-hmm."

"And, well . . . We heard Miss Sweet's name being bandied about in the mouth of that low-down character from back East."

Jenny gasped. "Ethan."

Allan nodded. "Yes, ma'am, I believe so. Teddy wanted to confront him, but I thought it better to tell Mr. Garrett and let him decide. I know we don't want your reputation sullied even a mite, but we also—"

"We can't risk having him come back and do worse to the herd," Lucas finished for him. "Criminy." He rubbed his chin thoughtfully.

"Yes, sir."

"You did just right, Allan, bringing this to me. Thank you."

"Do you want me to saddle Bo for you, sir?"

In that moment he made a decision.

"Actually, hitch up the wagon for us. We'll meet you out there in a minute."

Allan nodded and left, but when Lucas turned to Jenny she seemed bewildered.

"We need to go into town," he said. "We need to clear your name."

"I couldn't . . . They don't want to see me," she said, a little sadly. "And I'm fine with that, really. I have you and Mary and this whole place. I don't want to go into town if it means upsetting people."

"No, honey," he said gently, crossing to her and taking her hands again. "We can't let him think he can do whatever he wants. I know it's going to be hard, but we need to nip this in the bud."

"How are we going to do that? Ethan has been waging a full campaign against me for days. Longer!"

"I don't know yet, but I know that running from it won't solve anything. You and I have already learned that, haven't we?"

She sighed, looking up at him with trust and adoration in her eyes. "You're right. Tell me what you think we should do."

CHAPTER TWENTY-THREE

After leaving Mrs. Potter in charge of Mary and supper, Jenny changed into her nicest clean dress and prepared herself for a trip into Juniper Falls. Despite the fact that she could have lived the rest of her life without seeing Ethan again, she knew that letting the wound fester would only make the situation worse. She had tried running away, and that had only blown up in her face. The thing to do now was look straight into the mouth of the lion and show she was not afraid.

Lucas had promised not to leave her side, so when they arrived in town and he stopped the wagon outside the inn, she let herself be comforted. He took her hand and watched her quietly, waiting. The sun was just beginning to set and the warm light cast long shadows down the main street of Juniper Falls.

She took a deep, steadying breath.

"Are you afraid?"

Jenny looked at Lucas and offered him a brave smile. "A little. We don't know what else Ethan did after we left town the other day. He likely redoubled his efforts to sully my name and drive me from Juniper Falls."

"No one is going to drive you from Juniper Falls. Not if I have anything to do about it."

"Thank you." She smiled. "But there's still plenty of damage he can do by trying."

"Well, that's why we're here, isn't it? To stem some of the damage. The more the neighbors here know you, the less likely they will be to believe a word that man says."

"I hope you're right. I don't want you to be ostracized too."

"It won't happen. I promise you. The folks who live in this town are generous and welcoming. In fact, that may be why Ethan was able to get a foothold in the first place, right?" He squeezed her hand reassuringly.

She nodded.

"You let me go in first," he continued. "I want him to know that he's not going to be able to push you around because he thinks you're alone."

Jenny nodded again, grateful.

After squeezing her hand one more time, Lucas climbed down, helped her down, and then left her alone on the boardwalk in front of the inn. He was only gone a short moment before he reappeared, shaking his head.

"Mr. Brown said he wasn't in. Thought maybe the general store. Do you want to walk down there?"

Jenny was still not ready to speak, but she nodded and took his offered arm. As they walked the couple of blocks to the store, she told herself it was probably her imagination that made her think that people were staring at her. She kept her eyes looking right ahead, toward the task she had taken on.

Lucas ducked into the store quickly, then back out again to confirm that Ethan was inside.

"Let me, please," she said when her betrothed made offers and promises and claims about what he would do to the other man. "I don't want this to be a fight."

Lucas looked at her for a long moment before responding. "All right. But the moment he raises his voice at you . . ."

"I understand. I appreciate it."

She headed through the door to the general store and looked around. Ethan was grumbling in the center aisle. She didn't recognize the rough-looking man he was talking to, but judging from Ethan's gestures and expression, he was upset about something and his friend was commiserating. Jenny wanted to keep from making a scene; she wished he was not in the middle of the store. When she reached him, she quietly touched his elbow to get his attention.

"Ethan," she said in a low voice. "Can we talk?"

He whirled around at the sound of her voice and backed away from her so quickly he stumbled over his feet.

"I don't want to hear anything you have to say. I don't want you anywhere near me."

He turned to storm away, but his path was blocked by a curious onlooker—Tom Coulter, the blacksmith—standing at the end of the aisle and watching Ethan with a warning expression.

"I understand that you've been spreading more stories about me," she said in a calm voice. "I thought I made it clear that such behavior is unfair and ungentlemanly. I do not deserve to be treated that way at all, but especially not in my new home. Could you please just . . . Ethan. Just go back to Baltimore. Leave me to my life. You never have to see me again."

The door of the general store opened as more people heard the shouting and came to see what was wrong. Jenny realized she did not know which of these men watching might be the shopkeep.

"Throw her out!" Ethan yelled to the crowd that was gathering. "Is this the kind of person you want in your community? This wretched, selfish, useless woman?"

Jenny heard a gasp and felt a scarlet blush creep up her cheeks. She should have known better—a public place would not curtail his tongue at all. There was a fleeting moment where she realized she would need to grieve the loss of this friend from her life, on top of losing David, but that was not a thing she could deal with right now.

"Ethan," she said. "Let's talk about this. Let me go through the whole thing with you."

"I don't want your lies worming their way into my head," he spat at her. Turning to the room at large, he yelled, "Jenny Sweet is dangerous! She's going to get you all killed"

"Miss Sweet saved me," Teddy said in a clear, carrying tone.

A curious murmur rippled through the growing crowd. Jenny was shocked. She hadn't realized the ranch hand had followed them into town, but now the sweet young man was standing up for her, knowing he would soon be the target of Ethan's ire.

"She did!" Teddy insisted to the crowd, stepping further into the store. "We were fixing a fence and it slipped and the force of the rail jabbed into me. I broke a rib and tore up my side, and she was there through every bit of it. Nursing is not one of her duties at the ranch, but she made sure to dress my wound and look after me all the same. *And* when we had that storm a few weeks back, she was up out of bed helping with the rest of us. There's no doubt in my mind she has a kind heart and the best of intentions. Don't listen to this rabble-rouser."

Jenny had had a very emotional day already, and this capped it all. While she knew that Teddy appreciated her help with his injury, it never occurred to her that he could be an ally in her own troubles. She had come here with Lucas at her side to try to reason with Ethan, and she had found a new friend.

"Thank you," she said.

The more support she felt from the people of Juniper Falls, the more confident Jenny could be that this entire trouble would get sorted out. All was not lost when people looked out for each other.

————

After Jenny thanked Teddy for his kind words of support, there was a brief lull in the crowd. Everyone looked to Ethan Watts to see how he would take it. He had been trying so forcefully to rob her of any support that he seemed disbelieving that he had not succeeded. Lucas was trying to decide if he should say something or if he should let Jenny continue on her own, when another voice cut through the crowd.

"She helped me too," Daisy said.

Everyone turned to the far corner of the store where Daisy Lambert stood with her friend Edith, a basket of canning supplies over her arm. She looked embarrassed at the attention, but valiantly continued. "She doesn't even know me, but she dropped everything she was doing at that picnic to make sure I was all right. There's nothing that you can say that will make me believe she is callous to anybody else's pain."

Jenny seemed too overwhelmed to speak. All around them, the crowd was closing in, trying to get closer to the action and, in some cases, even moving to stand between Jenny and Ethan.

Lucas was so proud of her, he could burst. While he had been deeply committed to standing by her side and supporting her under the onslaught of Ethan's accusations, it had been too much to hope that anyone else would do the same. He had not even realized how much of an impression she'd made on the people of Juniper Falls in just a couple visits to town. He caught her eye and smiled, noticing how overwhelmed she still seemed.

Before he could do anything more for her, though, someone else spoke up.

"And she helped me with my own injuries. Future ones, that is," the blacksmith added with a self-deprecating laugh. "Miss Sweet took time out of her day to walk these very aisles with me, picking out dressing and ointment that I could have on hand in the event of burns and breaks in my forge. Even if we never need it, I like knowing that I'm prepared for the future. It was her idea, and she helped me see such planning would be far easier than I feared."

Tom grinned at Jenny, bowing dramatically to show his gratitude.

"Thank you," she whispered.

Ethan now was sputtering his protests—"You don't know her! You don't know what she could do!"—though no one paid him much mind. Lucas wanted nothing more than to pick that man up and bodily throw him from the general store, from Juniper Falls altogether, but he was better than that. Seeing the entire community come together to jointly reject the man's ire gave Lucas the confidence to speak up as well. Jenny would be all right. They both would.

"And she's helped my daughter learn to trust again," Lucas said, not taking his eyes off of Ethan. "At every turn, in every situation, she has been understanding, generous, and capable. It is so clear that she takes pleasure in helping those around her, I can't help but think Mr. Watts must be truly deluded if he cannot see it. And though my daughter has been without a mother for several years now, I have faith that under Miss Sweet's influence, she will never feel alone or uncared for.

"And I doubt we can say the same for you, Mr. Watts," he finished, stepping closer to the man and bringing to bear all his own heft and size to intimidate him. "Not with the poison you spew. You are making yourself miserable and I frankly feel sorry for you."

"I think you should probably go home, Ethan." Jenny stepped between him and Lucas. She was clearly trying to be kind to him, far more than he deserved. "Go home to your parents. Don't let your mother live any longer with both of her sons gone from her."

Ethan looked around angrily. Even the man he'd been

talking to earlier had abandoned him, disappearing into the crowd at some point during the disturbance.

The town had rallied around Jenny, and Lucas by extension, proving that a person's character was valued by their actions, not by what someone else might say about them. Lucas could not have been prouder of her, and could not have been prouder to be seen with her.

Ethan pushed through the crowd, stopping only to knock over a stack of boxes of ammunition that the shopkeeper, Mr. Thrush, had spent time setting up. He flailed wildly, evidently aiming to ruin as many people's days as he could until he got to the door of the store.

"Didn't know what a bunch of fools were out here in the West!" he yelled to those gathered. "You'll regret every bit of this, but it ain't my problem. I warned you!"

The crowd watched as he flung himself out the door, into the street, and away from Juniper Falls.

Lucas hung back for just long enough to watch Mrs. Langdon and Mr. Coulter come up to Jenny to comfort her.

He could not be more proud to be marrying this woman.

CHAPTER TWENTY-FOUR

By the time the crowd in the general store had dispersed some, Jenny felt like her heart rate had returned to normal. This second confrontation with Ethan and the unexpected kind words from her new neighbors had left Jenny feeling drained, but with the same satisfaction that came from a job well done. She managed to extricate herself from the pastor's wife and pull Lucas with her.

"Let's go outside a moment," she said. "I need air."

They stepped onto the boardwalk, and Jenny looked around nervously. Ethan had truly disappeared. While she knew he might be packing or hiring a stagecoach to the train station, she deemed it a positive sign that he was not on the street waiting for her. They seemed to have truly gotten rid of him.

She could feel Lucas watching her, concerned, and turned to ease his worry.

"Thank you for standing up for me," she said softly.

"I would wrestle a bear for you." He put his arm around her shoulders and squeezed her close to his side, heedless of all the people nearby. "Telling Ethan to leave town was easy. Now, though, what can I interest you in? We could go get supper at the Sunshine Cafe? We could look in at the seamstress for the new dress options you mentioned the other day?"

"I think I'd like to just go home—*our* home. If that's all right? Supper will be ready by the time we get there and we can have a quiet night together."

"Of course it's all right. Let me tell Teddy we're heading back and then I'll walk us back to the wagon."

As she waited for Lucas to return to her, Jenny looked around at the busy main street of Juniper Falls. It had been a difficult fight—both admitting to herself that this life was what she truly, deeply wanted, and also staking her claim to make sure it was not taken from her.

But now, heading home with this wonderful man, knowing that their path ahead was clear, Jenny realized it had all been worth it.

———

After the excitement of the afternoon, Lucas drove Jenny back to Prairie Winds Ranch, both of them talking about anything but the scene they had left behind. While Lucas would be open and available to Jenny if she ever wanted to talk about it, it felt right not to dwell on it now, to not give that man any more of their time or attention.

It was time for them to look forward; they had a ranch to run and a child to raise.

When he pulled the wagon into the yard, Allan was on hand to take care of the horses for them. That man wasn't much for gossip, but Lucas could tell that he had been lingering nearby. The relief on his face when he saw that Jenny had returned was evident.

"Teddy got back a little before you did," Allan said. "And Mrs. Potter said supper will be ready in about ten minutes."

"That's perfect," Jenny told him, gratefully. "Thank you so much."

As he led the horses to the barn, Lucas reached for Jenny, stopping her before she went into the house.

"I know you need to go help Mrs. Potter with supper, but if you have a moment, I would love to show you something."

Curious, Jenny nodded and followed Lucas across the yard.

He led her past the barn, around the chicken coop, and to the enormous bur oak tree where he had found so much comfort and clarity at other times of his life. Now, when he led his future wife to what had previously been such a private space, he was surprised to find that sharing it with her made it even more special. He wanted to let Jenny into the deepest parts of his heart. He was safe with her, and she with him.

What better place to begin the rest of their lives together?

"This is one of my favorite places on the ranch," he said as they walked hand in hand up to the tree. As he explained its significance and how this was where he'd been when he realized he loved her, she seemed to be drinking in every word with interest. "I wanted to make sure you knew it was here. And let you know where to find me sometimes."

"It's beautiful," she said, looking around in wonder. "Thank you so much for sharing it with me. I know it's a big deal to open up all parts of your life."

He watched her stroll around the trunk of the tree, her hand resting on the cool bark as she circled it.

"I'm glad you like it . . . I thought we could marry here."

She ran the last couple of steps around the tree trunk until she was in front of him again. "Here? Are you sure? Lucas, doesn't this spot mean too much to you?"

"You mean too much to me for me to keep it to myself any longer. I'm not saying we should build a second house here, or let the boys set up camp, but our most special day should be in a special place."

She looked around again, this time with an appraising look in her eye. Finally, she turned back to him. "I think it's perfect. I was never the kind of girl to dream about what my wedding might look like, but if I had, the shade of an oak tree that had been nurturing and guiding my beloved for years would be the perfect location."

He opened his arms to her and she stepped into them, a perfect fit against his body as though she'd always been meant to be there.

"I love you, Jenny Sweet. Bringing you to Juniper Falls has been the smartest thing I've ever done. I will never get tired of telling you so."

"I am so excited about our future together," she whispered.

"Me too."

He touched her chin, gently guiding her face up to his own as he kissed her.

EPILOGUE | FOUR MONTHS LATER

"Got something for you, Mrs. Garrett," Teddy said with a grin. He loped up the porch steps in just a few steps, handing over a letter.

"Oh! I had so hoped for this. Thank you so much."

"Ma'am." He tipped his hat and ran back across the yard to where Allan was unloading the wagon of the dry goods and gardening supplies that they'd collected in town.

Jenny and Lucas were enjoying the late afternoon sunshine on the porch of the ranch house after a long day of caring for the horses' hooves. Jenny was learning a lot about all that was required for ranching, and Lucas vowed that the animals were calmer in her presence than even his.

Ever since they'd gotten married, they had made a little ritual out of taking a late afternoon tea together. It offered the dual benefit of giving the couple a few minutes to rest in the midst of an otherwise chaotic life, and of giving them a few minutes to connect, to share details about their day and maintain that true friendship that had drawn them together.

Now they sat in matching rocking chairs, watching the hens in the chicken run across the yard and sipping lemon tea. Mary played with her paper dolls in the dirt at the foot of the porch steps and periodically called out to them to watch what she was doing. This daily respite had quickly become Jenny's favorite part of the day, and if one of the ranch hands showed up with mail for her, even better.

She set her tea down on the porch railing and tore open the envelope.

"Is that a letter from your sister?" Lucas leaned back in his chair, watching her with satisfaction.

Jenny laughed delightedly. "Eliza finally wrote. I'm surprised she sat down long enough to put pencil to paper, but I'm so glad she did."

"What does she have to say?"

"Promises to come visit. There might not be anything that comes of it, but I'm slightly more inclined to believe her this time. She's a painter, landscapes mostly, so the last time I wrote to her I was sure to tell her in as much detail as I could how beautiful Juniper Falls is."

"You know your family is always welcome. Might be nice if she came soon, for the Golden Days summer festival. That could keep her occupied while you and I are busy."

"Thank you. I miss them so much, and I think they would love it here, but of course they all have their own lives. If Eliza comes even for a little while, that will make me happy. She's the type to just jump at whatever the next interesting thing is, so if we can get her to come, we might have to be ready for her to leave at any moment."

"Write her back," he said, and drained the rest of his tea. "Either way, we are going to have the most perfect summer together."

————

Lucas watched his new wife pore over the letter in her hands. It didn't seem to be very long, only a couple sheets of paper, but she was enthralled with every word. He hoped for her own sake that Eliza would come to visit, but he also was confident that she was happy in her new life either way. Their wedding had been quiet and small, under the same tree where he often found solitude, and their life together had been peaceful ever since.

There would be no more solitude in his life, he realized. He didn't want to pull away from the world, not when he had this vision of kindness and grace at home waiting for him.

What more could a man want from life?

————

"Mother Jenny?" Mary called, coming around the side of the house to where they sat on the porch.

Jenny was still not used to being called "mother," but she and Lucas had agreed that the child needed something more familiar than Miss Sweet, and Jenny had no intention of taking her mother's place. Mother Jenny was the perfect compromise, and each time Jenny heard it she felt more at home in this new life.

"Yes, love, what is it?"

"Will you look at something for me?"

Mary held something small carefully in both hands, as though it were as delicate as an eggshell. While she still slept with the doll her mother had made her years earlier, over the month since her father had remarried, the doll's appearances became rarer by the day. Now, instead of clutching the doll to her wherever she went, Jenny more often found Mary with her hands dirtied by mud pies or learning to knead dough with Mrs. Potter.

And now she was carrying something with such focus and care that Jenny wondered what new adventure she was about to be plunged into.

"What've you got there, pet?" Lucas asked.

Not taking her eyes off the precious object she held, Mary came to stand between Jenny and Lucas. Peering over the edge of her tiny palm, Jenny saw a pink strawberry about the size of a marble.

"Do you see it?" Mary asked excitedly. "Do you think it's ready? There's three more like this on the strawberry plants. Can we pick them to put on pancakes in the morning?"

"Oh, love . . ." Jenny exchanged amused glances with her husband. "Thank you so much for keeping an eye on the vegetable garden for us, but I don't think this strawberry is ready to be eaten."

"Are you sure?" Mary looked up at her, eyes pleading. "But it's red, see?"

"It's . . . yes, well, it's on its way to turning red. That's true," Jenny said gently. "But they still have a few weeks to grow before they'll be as big and as sweet and as juicy as possible. Don't you want the very best strawberries we can grow? Even if it means we have to wait?"

"I suppose so."

"I'm sorry. I know you're disappointed. But I promise they'll be even better next month."

"I wish I hadn't have picked this one then."

"You can still eat it," her father offered.

"Lucas," Jenny protested with a laugh.

"It won't hurt her. Mary, if you want to, you can eat that little berry. And then just remember what it tastes like so you can compare it in a few weeks when we harvest the other ones."

Mary looked at Jenny, who shrugged. Lucas was right; it wouldn't hurt her, although she would not have been the one to suggest such a thing.

"Really?" she asked, as though she had not really believed she would be allowed to.

"Give it a try," Jenny said.

Mary's eyes seemed as big as saucers as she nibbled off every bit of the pinkish-red flesh she could, tossing the stem to the dirt. Her excitement quickly shifted and her puckered lips and shocked expression made Jenny and Lucas laugh.

"Yuck! *Yuck!* How come it tastes like that?"

"They'll taste better in a few weeks, I promise," her father said. "Why don't you go into the kitchen and see if Mrs. Potter will get you a glass of water or something to get the taste out of your mouth?"

Mary clattered into the house, the front door banging shut behind her.

"I'll have to have Allan check those hinges," Lucas

said thoughtfully after watching his daughter disappear. "She's getting big now, and will likely start leaving a trail of destruction in her wake."

"Well, where better for her to learn patience and carefulness than at home with us?" Jenny offered.

Her husband looked at her, holding her gaze with more admiration and affection in his eyes than she thought she could get used to.

"You know," he said, leaning forward and taking her hand in his. "I think placing that ad in Baltimore's paper might have been the smartest thing I've ever done."

"You've mentioned," she said with a grin. "Awfully smart of me to reply to it too, huh?"

"Mrs. Garrett, this bond we have is once in a lifetime."

"I quite agree, Mr. Garrett. Let's go sit under our oak tree."

———

Want to read Eliza's story?
Download *The Sweetest Spark* here
ATButler.com/SS02

She's chasing inspiration. He's running from his past. Together, they'll forge a love as unyielding as iron.

. . .

1881, Wyoming Territory: Eliza Sweet has always craved adventure, but her wanderlust has come at a price—leaving her without a place to call home. When she arrives in Juniper Falls, Wyoming Territory, to visit her sister, she's captivated by the untamed beauty of the West and determined to master the art of landscape painting. Yet her fiery spirit soon leads her to an unexpected encounter with the town's enigmatic blacksmith.

Tom Coulter prefers the heat of the forge to the company of others. A lonely man with a painful past, he's spent years burying his heart beneath iron and steel. But when Eliza bursts into his life with her vibrant energy and relentless curiosity, she sparks something in him he thought he'd lost forever.

As Eliza struggles to find her artistic voice and Tom battles the ghosts of his past, a simmering attraction ignites between them. But the closer they grow, the more Tom fears his pain will consume them both. When danger threatens their newfound bond, they'll need to trust each other—and the sparks between them—to forge a future together.

AUTHOR NOTE

Thank you so much for reading *The Sweetest Bond*. Whether you came to it because you love Romance, or because you love Juniper Falls, I'm grateful you're here.

I have a confession to make: This was my very first proper romance novel I have ever written. I read plenty of them, and to be honest I always thought I would enjoy reading them far more than writing them (I have the same feeling about cozy mysteries), I am so glad I took this risk.

I approach my books character first, figuring out the plot once I know better who my character is. And what I've learned from writing this book is that the romance genre is one of the most character-focused genres there is. You cannot possibly fall in love with another person unless you know them intimately, and I get to explore all of that and put it on the page for you.

I'm very much looking forward to introducing you to the other Sweet sisters as this series progresses. I also have a small seed of an idea to write another spin-off romance series about Teddy, Allan and possibly other future ranch hands that come to Prairie Winds Ranch (My editor called Teddy a 'golden Retriever' so that will definitely be a fun book to write).

I suppose that's the problem with writing these fictional towns filled with delightful characters—I am always so attached to them. I want to spend time with each and every one.

At the time of this writing, I also have a Juniper Falls women's fiction series launching this year—ATButler. com/jf-series. It features a family arrived from Philadelphia, a schoolteacher, a boarding house landlady and more. My hope is to build out this series (and other spin-off series) so we get to spend time with all the delightful personages of the ranching town.

This book had fewer historical notes for me to clarify, but one interesting thing is that I could not use the word 'triage' in the now-common medical way. According to Etymonline.com (my go-to resource), that word was not used to indicate sorting until World War I. Sticking to only the vocabulary in use at the time that the book takes place helps it feel authentic to the historical period in subtle ways.

Book two of the series—*The Sweetest Spark*—is Eliza's story as she comes to town and makes friends with the blacksmith. I hope you love it and thank you as always for your support!

— A.T. Butler
November 2025

MORE FROM JUNIPER FALLS

DOWNLOAD Traveling to Juniper Falls for FREE here

July 1882: Henry and Charlotte McBride, along with their spirited daughter Matilda, embark on a grand journey westward from Philadelphia to Laramie, Wyoming Territory, where they will be moving their whole life in Juniper 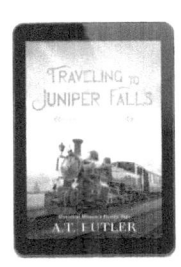 Falls. Their excitement is palpable as they settle into the rhythm of train travel, sharing stories, meeting fellow passengers, and watching the vast landscapes unfold before them.

But their smooth journey takes a hilarious and unexpected turn when one of their trunks—containing essential belongings—mysteriously vanishes at a station hundreds of miles too soon. The family must rely on quick thinking, a touch of luck, and the kindness of strangers to reunite with their misplaced possessions.

Perfect for fans of historical fiction with heart and wit, this delightful tale reminds us that sometimes, the best memories come from the most unexpected mishaps.

DOWNLOAD Traveling to Juniper Falls for FREE here

———

Stories from Juniper Falls {FREE}

Juniper Falls Series:
> *The Juniper Hotel*
> *Building the Dream*
> *Snowflakes and Sugar Cookies*
> *Prairie Storms*
> *Seeds of Change*
> *Golden Days*

Marrying a Sweet Sister Series:
> *The Sweetest Bond*
> *The Sweetest Spark*
> *The Sweetest Shelter*
> *The Sweetest Gamble*

ALSO BY A.T. BUTLER

Stories from Juniper Falls

<u>**Juniper Falls Series:**</u>
The Juniper Hotel
Building the Dream
Snowflakes and Sugar Cookies
Prairie Storms
Seeds of Change
Golden Days

<u>**Marrying a Sweet Sister Series:**</u>
The Sweetest Bond
The Sweetest Spark
The Sweetest Shelter
The Sweetest Gamble

<u>**Courage On The Oregon Trail Series:**</u>
<u>*Westward Courage*</u>
<u>*Faithful Trail*</u>
<u>*Frontier Sisters*</u>
<u>*Unyielding Heart*</u>
<u>*Wild Promise*</u>
<u>*Fierce Dreams*</u>

Seeking Home

Trouble and Grace

Oregon At Last Series:

Journey's End

Christmas in Oregon

Snowbound Promises

Pastor's Baby

Frontier Fortune

Reluctant Spring

Summer of Promise

Eden Valley Sunrise

Sweet Adventures

Jacob Payne, Bounty Hunter Series:

Trouble By Any Name

Danger in the Canyon

Justice for Jasper

Blood on the Mountain

Outlaw Country

Death By Grit

Desert Rage

Arizona Legend

Fool's Demise

Silent Night

Bountiful Justice Series:

Loyalty's Price

Riding for Justice

Trail of Redemption

Other Western Novels by A.T. Butler:

Hawke's Revenge

ABOUT THE AUTHOR

I grew up in the southwest—California Missions, snakes and constant threat of drought weaving the backdrop of my childhood.

But it wasn't until I moved to Texas a few years ago that the magic and mythology of the American West began to seep into my soul.

I'd love to write about western adventures, strong women and noble men for a long time.

If you enjoyed this book, a review on your favorite retailer would be greatly appreciated.

- A

www.ingramcontent.com/pod-product-compliance
Lightning Source LLC
Chambersburg PA
CBHW031443200726
48289CB00007BB/2181